Out Of Season

Out Of Season

by

Humphrey Brown

Nov. 97

So Judy
I hope you enjoy my
book.   Best wishes

Humphrey Brown

Audenreed Press

III

First Printing

Copyright © 1997
by Mary Ellen Brown

Cover Art by Mary Derr

ISBN   1-879418-83-5
Library of Congress Catalogue Card Number: 97-073439

Published in the United States of America by
Audenreed Press
Division of Biddle Publishing
P.O. Box 1305
Brunswick, Maine 04011
207-833-5016

Dedication

**To Gary, whose faith and inspiration
encouraged me to persevere
with this book.**

**A special thanks to my writer friends,
especially Betty
whose suggestions and support
helped so much.**

Thank you.

One

"Ah, smell that fresh air!" Roger beamed and held the door for Lady, his beagle, so she could go outside for her morning chores.

"What luck! Fresh snow. I waited all hunting season for snow, and now I get it. It *must* be a good omen. I can feel my luck changing. I sure picked the right day."

Roger ignored the cold air blowing on him and looked around the winter landscape. Early morning sunlight sparkled on the trees. For a moment, he forgot the long recession and his despair over employment.

Lady finished and ran back inside, squeezing between Rogers legs. Roger took one last deep breath to savor the crisp air, then he closed the door with a smile.

He made coffee as he always did since being out of work. While he waited impatiently for the water to boil, he studied the photo on the shelf above the coffee maker. It was a picture of his sailboat, *Happy Sails II U.* He remembered the day Emily snapped it just as he sailed into the cove. He smiled. *I sure hope I can keep you*, he thought, his smile fading as he wondered how he would pay for the boat's costs this coming season. It *was* his boat, after all, and it didn't seem right for Emily to pay for it.

He hoped Emily would leave quickly that morning, so he could put his plan into action. He was excited and a bit nervous. He'd never gone hunting out of season before, but reasoned things out carefully, thinking Emily would be proud of him, and she'd enjoy the venison. The recession had hit New Hampshire particularly hard, and if he couldn't find work, he'd still provide meat for the table. He <u>had</u> to.

Upstairs, the radio alarm clock went off. Emily reached to hit the off button after she realized Roger had already gotten up. *I knew morning was going to come too quickly.* She thought about the last time she looked at the clock—it had been nearly 3 AM. *Worrying about Roger*, she told herself, trying not to feel guilty about her excitement for tonight's big event.

Roger walked up to the bedroom with a cup of coffee in each hand. Emily brushed her long, blonde hair. She was slim and fit for a woman in her forties. Roger marveled as he admired her, then he handed her one of the cups.

"Thanks." She smiled back. "What'll you do today?"

He swallowed coffee. "The usual—check the paper and make some calls." He shrugged. "Don't worry. I'll keep busy."

Emily's eyes showed her sympathy. She understood his despair and wanted to help, which only made him feel worse.

"I'll be home by five today." She sipped her coffee. "I've got an important meeting this afternoon. I thought I'd wear my blue suit. What do you think?"

"It looks great on you, Em."

"You always say that." She turned to button her blouse and look in the mirror.

Roger set down his cup and came up behind her, encircling her with his arms. She smiled and leaned against him.

"You're so beautiful," he whispered.

She turned and kissed him. "I have to get going."

They lingered in an embrace for a moment, then Emily returned to her preparations.

Roger sighed. His heart beat quickly, filling him with excitement for his planned day. If Emily wasn't so concerned with her own agenda, she might have noticed his happy mood.

Emily was an accountant and worked from her home in an office Roger built in the breezeway between the house and garage. Roger was a carpenter, but, during the past year and a half, the recession dried up all his work.

"How about if I get the mail for you today?" he offered. "It'll save you some time."

"That would be great."

At eight-fifteen, Roger drove down their long driveway to the country road, then went the five miles to town to get their mail at the post office. They decided to use a post office box for Emily's business so they wouldn't have to worry about mail while they were away at their cottage in Maine.

Emily gathered her papers and prepared for her day. She was a very organized person, and by the time Roger returned, she was ready to leave.

She started her car, then rolled down the window to speak to Roger, who was waiting for her to leave. "Remember tonight," she said, "I'll pick up the tuxedo for you."

"I remember," he lied, leaning in to kiss her good-bye. "Don't worry. I'll be ready when you get back. Good luck with your meeting." He smiled and watched her back up, turn, and drive away.

Roger gulped. He forgot that tonight was Emily's big event. She was to be recognized for her help with the new building project for the local Boys' and Girls' Club. She donated time and assistance to put the project together, and she was happy to learn she would be honored at a dinner party with all the important people in the local community.

As Emily drove off, Roger hurried to put his scheme into action. First, he locked Lady in the garage. She would fuss and whine, then she'd quiet down. At least there weren't any close neighbors to hear her.

To lesson his minor guilt for locking her up for most of the day, he gave her some doggy treats. Lady was spoiled more than usual since Roger and Emily's children left for college a few years ago.

Lady looked up at him with sad dark-brown eyes, as if she understood something wasn't right.

"You'll be OK, Girl." Roger patted her head and closed the garage door. He didn't like locking her up, but, if he didn't, she'd follow him.

Ignoring the treats, Lady whined as soon as Roger closed the door.

Roger ran up the stairs two at a time. In the master bedroom, he got his Winchester 94 off the wall rack above the bureau. *This little baby will make all the difference*, he thought.

The rifle was a Christmas present. He would've bagged his buck during deer season if he had that gun. He set the rifle on the bed and reached for his hunting knife, strapping it around his chest with a thick leather belt. The knife was a birthday present from his son, Tony, but he never needed it before.

Somehow, this day felt special. He secured the top of the knife to his shoulder and the bottom of the knife to his belt with a narrow strap he cut from one of Emily's old leather handbags, then he put on his winter coat and green plaid hat. He eyed himself in the mirror. His worn jeans fit snugly, and his heavy boots were tied securely to keep his feet warm and dry. He held the rifle in front of himself and grinned at his reflection.

Then he heard a vehicle coming down the driveway. "Oh, no!" He looked out, and his stomach tightened. He set the rifle on the bed and ran downstairs.

A short, heavy-set man dressed in a dark blue three piece business suit was heading towards the door. It was Norman, one of Emily's clients, probably stopping by to drop something off.

"Shit. This isn't part of the plan. What if I was walking down the driveway with my rifle? I need to be more careful, or I'm going to blow it."

He glanced down to make sure his knife wasn't showing just as the doorbell rang. Roger took a deep breath and opened the door with a smile.

"How's it going, Norman?"

Norman was an older man who like to talk and was apt to hang around for an hour or more, especially when Roger was present. He knew Roger wasn't working and felt visiting was appropriate. "Good morning, Roger. Is Emily here? I've got some papers for her."

"You just missed her." Roger managed to hide his distress. "I was just heading out, too. I promised Smitty I'd help at the farm today."

Norman eyed Roger suspiciously, but he took the hint and left after fifteen minutes. He had an appointment, too.

Roger went back upstairs and got his gun. *I'll go out the back door and into the woods*, he thought. *No one will see me.*

His hands were shaking a bit, which amused him. He wondered if he'd go through with it, or if he was really just finding an excuse to do what he liked-- escape to the woods. *Why waste my time, there aren't any jobs?*

As he stepped out the back door, he glanced around. When he made sure he was alone, he walked toward the forest behind the house, holding his Winchester close to his side, as if hiding it from view. Lady barked as he walked away, begging to be included in the adventure.

Once in the woods, Roger calmed down. It was a beautiful winter day, with sunlight glistening on the new snow. Tree branches were heavily laden with it. He picked his way carefully through the woods, passing old fallen trees and white-laced evergreens, heading for a well-known spot.

He studied the ground as he walked, seeing many deer tracks and droppings. Soon, he reached his favorite tree. There were lots of tracks and deer signs all around it, making it look like the gathering place for the entire herd.

With fresh snow everywhere, Roger could almost see what the deer did during the night. He imagined them gathering under the tree and in nearby bushes. They nibbled on shoots and branches in the thicket, and they left indentations on the ground where they lay during the night.

As he climbed into the large pine tree, he felt nervous again. Emily should be away for another four hours. If all went well, he'd have enough time.

The sun warmed his face as he sat on a comfortable limb. He removed his hat and ran his fingers through his thinning brown hair. He scratched his neatly-trimmed beard and yawned, then he thought about his previous close encounters with **the buck** he so desperately wanted during hunting season. He was so comfortable, he almost dozed.

As he sat there, he thought about what he was doing. He never broke the law before, but, somehow, this was different. He hunted that buck for three seasons, although this was the first year he seriously pursued it.

In the past, he used an old shotgun. It was a good gun for bird hunting, but, for bigger game, it was almost useless. One day, after hunting season, he tested the gun's accuracy with Smitty, his neighbor who ran the farm down the road. Both men were surprised at how far the bullet was from the target. It varied as much as three feet. That was when Roger decided to get a Winchester 94. Emily agreed, suggesting it as a Christmas present.

He enjoyed being outdoors, and the fact that he hadn't gotten his buck in past years didn't bother him. This year, he went hunting every day, because it was suddenly more important. He **had** to have that buck.

Smitty told Roger how the deer destroyed his apple trees and caused untold numbers of automobile accidents. All that added to Roger's rationalization about hunting that buck, but one other factor pushed him to the decision.

He and Emily visited some friends who hunted, too. Both of them, husband and wife, got a deer that season, and Emily raved over how good the venison tasted. Roger felt he had to bag that elusive buck. It was a matter of pride. He never shot a deer before, but he wanted Emily to know he was still virile.

As he sat on the limb, he knew Emily would never have agreed to him hunting out of season, but he felt certain she'd forgive him once he showed her the venison. He could convince her—after the fact.

An hour passed, and Roger wondered if he was making a mistake. Perhaps he should come back on another day, later in the week. He looked at his watch. It was already one-thirty, and his stomach gurgled. He forgot to bring a lunch.

"I hope that deer won't be frightened away by my noisy stomach," he muttered.

Another hour passed. It was two-thirty, and he seriously considered going back. *What if Emily comes home early for some reason*? he wondered.

His pulse quickened. He could always hide his rifle in the woods and pretend he was out for a walk, then retrieve it later. Feeling better after making that decision, he waited a little longer.

"I'll leave at three," he said. "No matter what."

Fifteen minutes later, he heard something crunching and snapping below. Something was walking, and he estimated it was one hundred yards away. It might be a deer—perhaps even his buck.

He strained to see through the trees. The New England winter sun was low in the sky, and shadows filled the thicket. He listened intently as the noises came closer, but he still couldn't see the deer.

It's got to be close, but where? he wondered.

As he tried to locate the source of the sound, it occurred to him to look behind him. The noise was coming from the opposite direction, not directly toward him as he first thought. He'd have to get closer to see the deer and shoot it.

He sat silently for a moment, listening. Sure enough, the sounds continued.

It's pretty noisy, he thought. *Maybe the deer aren't so fearful with hunting season over*.

He climbed down as quietly as he could and walked slowly toward the sound. He clicked off the safety on his rifle, and cocked the hammer. His heart pounded, and his breath came rapidly.

He picked his way through the thicket, listening for his buck. The new snow was only an inch deep, and dry twigs underneath cracked when he stepped on them. He paused every few steps to listen, noting that the buck was stopping and listening, too. The noises were irregular.

It probably hears or smells me. He tried to determine if there was a breeze and where it came from.

The snapping and cracking came closer. Roger neared a small clearing along a wide trail. In deep snow, snowmobilers used that trail.

A man's camouflage hat moved above the bushes, and Roger's heart jumped. He hadn't been stalking a buck, it was a man! He stood rigid and still, and watched the hat.

There was a large boulder to his left. Roger quickly placed his rifle behind it. The man might be a game warden, and Roger didn't want to be caught hunting out of season.

He tried to breathe slowly to calm himself. Then, with his fists nervously clenched, he walked toward the stranger, assuming the man probably saw him already. The only person he could imagine who might be walking around on his property was the game warden. If the man asked, Roger would say he was out taking a walk.

The man wore green camouflage pants and jacket and black military boots. He was almost six feet tall, with a slight build. Despite the snug design of his clothing, it fit loosely on him.

When they were fifty feet apart, Roger called, "Hey!"

The man turned without seeming surprised. Roger gulped. *He looks like he's expecting me*, he noted. The man's face was dark with beard stubble, and he seemed pretty unkempt for a game warden. Roger didn't recognize him at all.

*What's he doing out here if he's **not** a warden?* Roger wondered.

"You're early." The man spoke with a low, gruff voice and motioned. "Come here."

"Uh-oh," Roger muttered. "I'm up shits creek now." He walked forward and tried to act nonchalant. The man **had** to be a game warden. Roger tried not to look guilty.

At forty feet, the man reached inside his jacket, and Roger's steps slowed. He watched the man pull out a 9 mm handgun with a silencer on the barrel.

Roger froze, filled with fear and indecision. He couldn't grasp what was happening, but the urge to do something was strong. *What kind of warden uses a gun like that?* he wondered. *Is he planning to arrest me?*

The gun fired softly, and Roger stumbled backward and fell. Something hit his chest like a sledgehammer. He turned to run just as another shot stung him under the right arm and splintered a small tree in front of him. Roger gasped in disbelief. The man intended to kill him!

He ran, slipping in the snow and trying to catch himself as he raced toward the boulder where he left his rifle. Then he saw it. He glanced back at the man, then dived, landing in the snow on top of his

Winchester 94. He trembled as the man came up behind him.

"Wait a minute," Roger said. "What are you doing?"

The man walked forward with a sinister grin on his face, his gun aimed at Roger. Roger's heart beat so hard, he felt it might burst. His breath came in gasps, and his hands felt clammy.

Roger clenched his teeth, expecting to die at any second with another bullet in him.

My Winchester! He rolled over and raised the rifle. It fired almost without any effort on his part. The attacker fell, shot between the eyes.

Stunned, Roger stared at the fallen body. Adrenaline surged through him, making him giddy. He wasn't sure if he felt joy at being alive or perverse pleasure at hitting his target.

"Oh, my God." He repeated the phrase several times as he stood up. Dizzy and nauseous, he stumbled to a stump and sat with his head between his hands, trying not to pass out. "Oh, my God!"

When the dizziness passed, Roger tried to evaluate the situation. Pain throbbed in his abdomen, and the wound in his arm stung and burned. Using his left hand, he unzipped his coat and slid his right arm out, then his left. The jacket fell to the ground. His heart beat rapidly as he wondered what he'd find. His shirt was bloody, but not as much as expected.

As he removed his hunting knife, he discovered why he was still alive. The first bullet hit his knife and was lodged in the blade. There was a large, long bruise outlining the shape of his knife on his chest. The second bullet grazed the inside of his left arm below the armpit. That wound bled a lot, but it didn't seem that serious.

He tied his scarf around his arm and put on his coat, then he walked to the dead man. He kept his rifle in front of him just in case the man moved, but he didn't.

There was a hole in the man's forehead. Using the rifle butt, Roger moved the man's head and saw the exit wound. It was larger than the entry wound, but it wasn't that big.

"I can't believe this." Stunned, he tried to gather his thoughts. He wanted to run, but he forced himself to remain and think. *Why did he want to kill me?* he wondered. *What do I do now?*

He searched the man's pockets for identification. There was a wallet, which he quickly opened. He looked away, fearful of what he might find. The situation was so bizarre, the man just might be a game warden. Roger clung to his sanity.

They'll say I was temporarily insane, he thought weakly.

He visualized his trial and sentencing like a man who sees his life passing before his eyes just before death. The analogy made him chuckle. *Will it be permanent insanity?* he wondered.

"How can I tell the authorities?" he muttered. "They'll want to know why I was out here with a rifle out of season. They'll charge me with murder. Emily would be embarrassed. It would hurt her business and social standing. I can't do that to her."

Then he remembered the honorary dinner planned for that evening. "I can't ruin her special night. I can't humiliate her."

He took a deep breath and looked in the wallet. There was a driver's license, several fifty and one hundred dollar bills, and five credit cards. The name on the license was Brian Gustafson from White Plains, New York. The picture matched the corpse. His dark greasy hair was tied in a short ponytail. He had a dark complexion, brown eyes, and a week's growth of beard. To Roger, the man looked like evil incarnate.

Roger read the credit cards without noting that each one was new and issued to a different name. He stuffed the wallet back into the man's pocket.

As he stood over the body, he thought he heard some noise in the woods. He looked up, fearing someone might be watching from the trees or be walking down the path. There were snowmobile trails everywhere in the woods, and people went cross-country skiing on them, too, but with so little snow, it wasn't likely he'd see anyone on a weekday. At this moment, he wasn't sure of anything.

Roger attached his knife to his waist and left his rifle in the snow. He buttoned his coat gingerly, trying not to press too hard on his bruised abdomen.

Then he remembered the old well on the south side of his forty acres. It was about a hundred yards away. The neighbors urged him to fill it in last summer so no one would fall in, but he never got around to it. Now he was glad he hadn't.

It took all his strength to hoist the 200-pound body to his back. Roger wasn't a big man, but he was muscular. Even so, carrying that heavy corpse was difficult. By the time he reached the well, he was sweating profusely. He lowered the body to the base of the well and wiped his brow with his sleeve as he gasped for breath.

He knelt and pushed aside the old wooden cover, then he reached into the well with a long branch. The hole went down at least eight feet. When he brought the stick up, it was wet on the first two inches. Most of the well was filled with loose rocks and leaves.

Roger decided to slide the body in head first. "Sorry about this." He reached for the dead man.

It was harder than he thought. The man seemed more heavy than when he carried him. The body kept getting stuck on rocks and twigs along the well's walls. Roger had to pull and twist the body inch by inch down into the well.

Finally, it fell free. Roger grimaced as the body slid to the bottom of the well. The man's boots were three feet below the rim. Roger covered them with leaves and sticks, then he replaced the old cover as best he could.

He stood and looked around. Anyone could see that the area had been changed. The snow was messed up, and the area around the well was covered with dirt and footprints. There was heavy rain forecast for the evening, and Roger hoped the site would look more hidden in the morning.

He smoothed out the ground with some spruce boughs, but that didn't help much. By then, it was five o'clock and almost dark.

Two

Roger stood back and viewed the area one last time. He frowned, then ran back to retrieve his rifle. It was so dark by then, he had to feel for it in the snow.

"Where is it?" He clawed the ground, then he found it and stood.

He squinted at his watch and pressed a button on the side. "Holy shit!" It was past five o'clock, and Emily would be home soon.

Roger sprinted to the dark house, thankful Emily was late. He let Lady out of the garage and she whined, running around him, grateful to be free. Ignoring the dog, Roger hurried inside and rushed up to the bedroom, turning on the lights along the way.

Once in the master bedroom, he set his rifle beside the shower, then removed his bloody clothes. Lady followed him upstairs. She started to bark, alerting him that Emily was home. He turned on the shower, hoping Emily would assume he was dressing for their evening out.

He heard her open the door and greet Lady, who had trotted downstairs.

"Hi, Girl. You sure are glad to see me, aren't you? Where's Roger?" She patted the dog, listening as if she expected an answer. "Oh. He's in the shower."

Roger picked up his dirty clothes and hid them in the bottom of the hamper where he could dispose of them later. He sneaked into the bedroom and replaced his Winchester in the rack. The knife was still dirty and in its leather sheath. He didn't have time to take care of that.

He heard Emily coming up the stairs and set his knife on the floor and kicked it under the bureau. He raced into the shower just as Emily entered the bedroom.

"Hi, Honey!" she called.

"Hi, Em. You home?"

"I've got your tuxedo. I'll leave it on the bed." She walked over to place it on the bed. Her foot brushed the knife under the bureau, but she didn't notice.

Roger listened intently as Emily went back downstairs. Lady came into the bathroom and sat, looking at him as he held the shower curtain aside to listen. He looked down at the dog and their eyes met.

"What are you looking at?"

Lady stood, then turned and followed Emily downstairs.

Emily went to her car to get her briefcase and the new outfit she bought for the reception. She hoped Roger liked it and wanted to put it on soon. She was excited about the festivities that evening and checked the time. They had an hour to get ready.

While Emily was busy, Roger gingerly washed the flesh wound under his arm. As long as he didn't raise his arm, Emily probably wouldn't notice it.

He finished and turned off the shower just as Emily came upstairs with her new outfit in hand. Roger put on his bathrobe and walked out of the bathroom.

"What have you got there?" He glanced at her packages.

"It's a surprise. You'll have to wait until I'm done dressing. That's why I'm so late." She smiled. "I hope you don't mind?"

"Of course not. I can't wait to see it." He saw the tuxedo and winced. Then he noticed the edge of his knife showing under the bureau. He watched nervously as Emily took some things out of her drawer, her foot close to the knife. She smiled and walked past him on the way to the bathroom.

"You'll have to be patient. It'll take a while."

"That's OK, Dear. Take all the time you need."

As soon as she shut the bathroom door, Roger hurried over and kicked the knife farther under the bureau, making sure it was well-hidden. *I hope she doesn't notice it's missing from the rack*, he thought, noticing the knife's anchors were conspicuously empty.

He dressed slowly, not very happy about wearing a tight-fitting tuxedo, especially with the soreness of his wounds. The last time he wore one had been at their wedding twenty-five years earlier. His preferred attire was jeans and sweat clothes, and he protested loudly when Emily suggested he wear a tuxedo this evening. Suddenly, he was glad, because it had caused her to be late.

He clutched the bureau for stability as he recalled the horrible moment when Gustafson came at him. He visualized the body in the well and shuddered. "Oh, God," he whispered. "What have I done?"

When Emily came downstairs, Roger was just finishing his second beer. He watched the early news while he waited for her, wondering if he might hear something about the man.

Emily looked spectacular. She wore a short blue velvet cocktail dress that flattered her figure. "Wow, Em. You look great."

"Do you like it?" She turned slowly. "Tell the truth. How do I look?"

Roger noticed she had her hair done, too. Usually, she wore it straight, but tonight it had extra bounce and curl, and it seemed to sparkle in the light. Her eyes matched the deep blue of her dress. Roger thought she was gorgeous!

"I love it." He put his arms around her.

"Wait! You'll mess me up. Save it for later." She held him away with outstretched arms. "We have to go—I don't want to be late for my own dinner."

Roger felt rejected, but Emily smiled, and kissed him.

"There'll be news people at the dinner," she explained. "I want to look my best in case my picture's in the paper. It could happen." She giggled.

He smiled. "I guess so." He wasn't even thinking about the dinner party. His thoughts were on his getting arrested. He imagined a picture of himself in the paper with the headline, *Local Man Sought for Murder*.

"Emily gathered her purse and jacket. "Let's go."

He glanced at her. "You know, there's something to be said for being fashionably-late."

Emily gave him an I'm-not-amused look.

"I'll be right there," he said.

At the banquet hall, they were greeted by an usher and escorted to a large table where several other honored guests were waiting. Emily knew everyone and introduced Roger. He smiled and acknowledged each one.

"Relax, Roger," she whispered. "These are my friends."

"How long does this shindig last?" he whispered back.

"They haven't even served dinner yet." She smiled to hide her annoyance.

Norman came by to say hello to everyone at the table. He was a city alderman in his spare time and tented to overestimate his social status in the community.

After greeting everyone, Norman only nodded at Roger, and Emily noticed with concern.

"What's up with Norman?" she whispered.

"What do you mean?"

"He was awfully cool toward you. Have you offended him?"

Roger shifted in his seat. "Thanks, Em. Now I'm the idiot who offends your clients."

Emily didn't reply, and looked around hoping no one overheard.

After talking to someone else, Norman came back. "You look smashing tonight, Emily."

"Thank you, Norman."

"Did you get the papers I dropped off this morning?"

"Papers?" Emily glanced at Roger.

"They're on the kitchen table," he replied.

Emily looked at Norman. "I got home at the last minute. I'll look at those first thing in the morning."

Norman nodded. "No hurry." He eyed Roger. "Did you get to wherever you were going in such a rush this morning?" There was a hint of chiding in his voice.

Roger realized he had indeed offended the man earlier that morning. "Sure. No problem."

"Where was that?" Emily asked.

"Uh...I...." Roger was stumped for a good answer, forgetting that he told Norman he was going to help Smitty.

"He probably went hunting again, Norman," Emily teased. "All he thinks about these days is that big buck."

Roger cringed. "Emily, I did not go hunting!" He spoke each word distinctly.

"I certainly hope not," Norman said. "The season ended last week. Anyone caught in the woods with a loaded rifle now faces up to one year in prison and a fine of ten grand." He eyed Roger suspiciously.

Roger gulped and forced a smile. Emily was surprised to see him blushing.

The master of ceremonies stood to begin the evening's proceedings, and Norman returned to his table, to Roger's relief.

Emily received a plaque for her part in helping with the new youth center. She spoke briefly, thanking the community, then she glanced at Roger. "I especially want to thank my husband, Roger, who is always so supportive of my endeavors."

Roger felt awkward as people looked at him. The man beside him spoke up once the program ended.

"You're Emily's husband? What do you do?"

"I'm a carpenter."

"That's kind of slow, with the recession, isn't it?"

"You could say so."

"How'd you two meet?"

Roger smiled. "I was remodeling a building where she worked." He remembered the first time he saw her. She stood near a desk, and their eyes met briefly. She smiled at him, and he was immediately in love.

Roger was thankful Emily didn't ask any more about Norman as they drove home. She was unusually quiet.

Lady greeted them as they went inside. Emily set the plaque on the counter. "I'm going to bed. I'm beat."

"I was proud of you tonight. You looked great. Helping the community was a nice thing to do. I know how hard you worked on that project."

Emily smiled gratefully. "Thanks."

"How about a glass of champagne to celebrate your award?"

"That sounds nice." She put her coat on the back of the sofa and sat on a chair while Roger went to the refrigerator and got out a bottle.

He popped the cork and poured two glasses. "To the best wife in the world."

"To the best husband." Emily smiled.

The next morning, Roger made coffee while Emily showered. As she dressed, she chatted about the meetings of the previous day, explaining her new assignments. She took out a document describing her contract from her briefcase and showed it to him.

"Tell me what you think."

He didn't respond. His concentration wandered, and he barely glanced at the paper.

"Aren't you listening?"

"Sorry, Em. I heard you." He took the paper and tried to study it, but his lack of concentration bothered him. He hoped he was covering it up.

"How about if we go over this after breakfast?" He looked up at her quickly. *I must be losing my mind*, he thought.

Emily looked at him. "Is everything all right?"

"Yes. I'm just hungry. Let's eat."

"In a minute. I need to get something." She went back into the bathroom.

A few minutes later, she called, "What happened to your clothes?"

"What?" Roger was already downstairs in the kitchen.

"Your shirt in the hamper has blood on it! What happened? Are you all right?"

"Oh. That's nothing." Panic set in as he tried to think of a good, believable excuse.

She stood in the loft overlooking the kitchen. "What happened?"

"Oh, well...I tried to play a trick on Lady. You know, like I always do?" He chuckled. "I climbed up a tree and hid. It was funny watching her try to find me, but I fell and cut my arm when I crashed through the branches."

Emily peered over the balcony at him with wide eyes. "Are you all right? Let me see." She started down the stairs.

"It's nothing, Em. I bandaged it, and it's fine. It bled a lot. I was going to tell you later. I didn't want to upset you."

"I'd still like to take a look." She walked over to him.

Roger insisted he was all right, so she reluctantly turned and went back upstairs into the bedroom to finish getting ready.

I was pretty clever, thinking up that excuse, he thought. *I hope Emily believed it.* For a brief moment, he fantasized that he'd actually been playing with Lady that afternoon.

Then the image of the dead man came to his mind. Roger dropped the glass he was holding into the sink. Luckily, it didn't break. He waited to see if Emily heard him.

He went back to preparing breakfast. *I have to get a grip on myself!*

Despite what happened the previous afternoon, Roger had a hearty appetite. Maybe he was being heartless. Nonetheless, he enjoyed his breakfast with Emily and savored the normalcy of it, hoping life would stay that way. He kept fearing his happy life would be shattered by the discovery of his terrible deed.

When they finished, Roger and Emily cleaned up the kitchen together, then Emily went into the office to organize her day. Roger used the time to finish cleaning his messy clothes and put them in the washer. He did the laundry often enough so it wouldn't seem that unusual.

As he worked around the house, he mentally reviewed the events of the previous afternoon. Something was bothering him, but he couldn't recall it. He sensed he was overlooking something and now wished he'd looked more carefully at the dead man's wallet, and felt sorry he hadn't taken it to find out more about the man.

He planned to go get it as soon as he could. That would also give him the chance to make sure the body was well concealed.

Emily spent the day in her office while Roger did his own work. He ran some errands and got their mail. On the way, he noticed the blue car for the first time. It was parked alongside the road near the end of their driveway, out of sight from the house. They passed it the previous evening, but he hadn't paid any attention.

Around six o'clock, Emily came into the house from her office. Roger built a fire in the fireplace, and set out two wine glasses. He didn't want Emily getting involved in the murder and hoped to reassure her everything was fine. He didn't want her to become suspicious and start asking questions.

They relaxed in front of the fire and sipped wine. Then the phone rang—it was Tony, their son. When the conversation ended, they compared notes on the call to assess his happiness. "How did he sound to you?" "Fine." It was a ritual to which they'd grown accustomed since their children left home a few years ago.

They watched a movie Roger brought home from the video store, then they went to bed at eleven. Roger was tired from all the work and stress and fell asleep in just minutes.

At three o'clock in the morning, he woke with a start and sat bolt upright. *Oh, no!* he thought. *Where is the gun? I left Gustafson's gun in the woods! I should've thrown that into the well, too. I knew I was forgetting something!*

Emily stirred beside him so he decided to sleep on the couch so he wouldn't disturb her. Besides, he was too agitated to sleep.

He sat in the dark and thought about the gun. It must have dropped somewhere near the boulder where Gustafson fell. He had to get it before someone else did. He retraced the events of the previous afternoon—every detail was clear in his mind.

It was dark just before dawn, with a steady rain outside. The sound gave Roger some solace, because it would was away much of the evidence. *It might also expose the gun*, he thought considering getting a flashlight and searching for it in the dark.

That would be too hard to explain to Emily if she woke, besides, he'd be soaked by the time he got back. She would be sure to notice that.

Roger berated himself for being so stupid. *How could I think I could get away with hunting out of season?* he wondered. *Venison on the table! Did I really think that would prove my manhood to Emily?*

He shook his head as he remembered how he had fantasized and rationalized. Smitty, with that knowing wink of his, had told him he should get the buck before someone else did. Why had he thought Smitty knew something he didn't? They often discussed with a disdain, real or pretend he wasn't sure now, those men who shot deer without tagging them. Did they really get away with it, or was it just some sort of macho bragging?

Perhaps the most compelling argument was the game warden who visited them after hunting season to check on a moose in the area. He told Roger and Emily it was the worst year yet for deer-related automobile accidents. "Overpopulation," he'd said, shaking his head. "Over a thousand accidents—there are just too many deer."

All that encouraged Roger to make his fateful decision to go after **the buck** out of season, something he never did before. **The Buck** that seemed to mock him all during hunting season. If only he could turn back the clock and rethink his actions.

Who was Gustafson? He wondered. *What was he doing here, and why did he want to kill me?*

There was no answer. He would always remember the way Gustafson looked at him as he took aim. The man intended to kill him, but why? He never saw Gustafson before.

Finally, at five o'clock, Roger went back to bed and fell asleep.

The alarm went off at six-thirty. Startled by the noise, Roger jumped out of bed.

Emily laughed. "You must've been in a deep sleep."

Roger sat down on the bed—his body aching from his troubled night. When Emily went into the bathroom, he reached for his missing knife under the bureau, removed the sheath, and wiped the blade on his pajamas, then placed it back on the gun rack.

Satisfied everything looked normal, he said, "I'm going downstairs to make the coffee."

"I can do that this morning," Emily called through the bathroom door. "You look tired."

"That's OK."

She shrugged and got into the shower. *I hope he's all right*, she thought. *He'll feel better once work picks up. I sure hope it's soon.*

Roger thought hard as he made coffee. He would go back into the woods after Emily left for an errand. *I just hope she has something planned.*

He let Lady out and smelled the moist, wet air. It seemed too warm for January—such a change from just two days ago. After Lady came back in, he fed her, and poured two cups of coffee. So deep in thought, he put two teaspoons of sugar into Emily's cup and none into his own.

"I should've called the police," he muttered, reaching for the cream. "Now I really look guilty. I'll never be able to prove it was self-defense."

He thought what he could've done besides hide the body. Maybe someone was looking for Gustafson; maybe he had a family, children, or a pet waiting for him.

Then he remembered the face—it was the meanest, ugliest face he ever saw. "Self-defense," he whispered.

"What did you say?" Emily asked from behind him.

"What?"

"What did you say? You were talking to yourself when I came in." She was sorry she surprised him.

"Nothing." He handed her a cup and sat with her at the breakfast bar.

Emily sipped her coffee and made a face. "How much sugar did you put in here? It's too sweet."

Roger sipped his coffee and realized he must've put his sugar into her cup. "I'll make you a fresh cup." He dumped her coffee into the sink and made a new one.

Emily watched curiously.

Roger felt as if someone else was controlling his body. He was like a robot, going through the motions of life without living them. He wondered if he'd lose his mind and felt like he might suddenly blurt, "I killed a man!"

He swallowed. Perhaps it was just his conscience, or it might be the beginning of real insanity. Deep in thought, he wondered if he'd ever regain the guilt-free state he once had.

"What would you like for breakfast?" Emily asked.

He wanted to say nothing, but to avoid arousing her suspicions, he said, "Just toast and juice."

While they ate, Emily made small talk about the upcoming visit they planned with her brother, George and his companion, Helen.

"I hope this January thaw ends before the weekend," she said. "It would be nice to have fresh snow for them. Maybe we could do some cross-country skiing."

Roger paused while chewing his toast. "George and Helen?"

"Oh, Roger, don't tell me you forgot? I can't believe it. We've been planning this for weeks."

"Of course not. I just forgot it was this weekend." Perhaps the visit would distract him. That would be welcome.

Roger showered and prepared for the day. Ordinarily, he would've had work to do until he was called back to work in the early spring. He was a finish carpenter with a construction crew, but, unfortunately, he'd been laid off longer than usual because of the extended recession.

He drove down the long driveway, completely distracted by thoughts of how to get back to the murder site without Emily knowing. Their home was far enough back from the road that it wasn't visible.

As he entered the roadway, he saw the same dark-blue Ford Escort parked nearby. It leaned halfway into the ditch, and it didn't belong to any of the neighbors. His heart raced when he realized who must've parked it there. *Oh, no! They'll know he was here!*

He slowed down and looked in the rearview mirror, but didn't dare stop and risk being seen near the car. It had been there for two nights—there was still some unmelted snow under it.

He glanced into the woods and saw nothing that would indicate where Gustafson entered. The heavy rain melted most of the snow.

Good, he thought. *Maybe there'll be no sign of his tracks.*

A green pick-up truck came up from behind and beeped. Roger looked in the rearview mirror and saw it was Smitty. Roger waved, sped up, and continued on his way.

As he drove to the post office, he kept thinking about the car, wondering if the police would come to investigate. *What about dogs?* he wondered. *Will they bring bloodhounds that can track a man for days after he disappeared*? He hoped no one reported the car for a while.

After he got back home, Emily kidded him about the coffee he made. She made them fresh coffee, and Roger laughed with her. They worked on separate projects until lunchtime.

The rain subsided, and Roger decided to take Lady for a walk and, hopefully, retrieve the gun. Emily was busy and skipped their customary lunchtime walk that day.

"Don't fall out of any trees." She watched Roger and Lady head into the woods.

Roger retraced his steps to the boulder where he shot Gustafson and searched intently for the handgun. It was tedious work because wet leaves covered the ground everywhere.

Finally, he stood near the boulder and retraced his steps to the spot where Gustafson fell.

"It has to be here." He kicked leaves aside, then got down on his knees and raked the ground with his fingers. Unsuccessful, he stood back up.

He headed toward the well, hoping to get Gustafson's wallet. As he walked, he watched the ground intently, wondering if the gun had been dropped along the way, and kicked at leaves to see if it was hidden. There was no sign of the gun.

The site looked good. He hated to disturb it after the rain did such a good job of hiding his previous marks.

He pulled off the well cover and brushed leaves aside until he saw the man's boots. It would be almost impossible to pull him out of the well, so he braced himself on his knees and reached for Gustafson's pockets.

Beep! Beep! Beep!

Roger jumped and knocked his head against the well's rock wall. "Holy shit!" He rubbed his head. "What the hell is that?"

He reached around the man's belt and found a beeper, which he unclipped. He stood up and examined the message flashing on the display. There was a number and a brief message – *Change of plans. 8:30, my office. JJ.*

Roger glanced around, feeling he was being watched. He fumbled until he shut off the beeper and listened for a moment. Satisfied no one was there, he bent down into the well again.

He reached into the pockets of Gustafson's Army jacket and saw something fall out, maybe a small creature, like a mouse, because of the way it moved. He jerked his hand away, then noticed something blue a little farther into the well, perched on a rock. Roger strained and barely managed to grab it. It was a tightly-tied dark velvet pouch which he slipped it into his own pocket.

He continued his search and finally found the wallet. That went into his pocket along with the beeper and the blue velvet pouch. He quickly pulled out of the well and covered the boots with more leaves and twigs.

When he replaced the cover, he was glad to see he hadn't left any obvious traces of his visit. He called Lady back from chasing a squirrel and started toward home.

He walked in through the front door to avoid Emily, who was in her office. Lady followed at his heels and jumped into an old chair reserved just for her. Roger stepped into the kitchen and hesitated, wondering where to hide the things he brought home.

He opened the basement door and went down the stairs, into the family and fitness room he'd built out of half of the basement, with a laundry room just outside. He looked around, trying to think of a good hiding place, then went into the laundry room.

This won't work, he thought. *Emily's apt to find something in here.*

He examined the cupboards near the washer and dryer, then went into the unfinished part of the basement. When he looked up, he smiled. *This'll do fine.*

He hid the wallet, beeper, and pouch above one of the beams. After studying it for a second, he was satisfied no one would discover the hiding place.

He went upstairs to see Emily. Lady jumped off her chair and followed Roger to the back door. Emily was busy in her office and glanced up, and smiled. "I see you've been playing with Lady again."

Roger looked down at this dirty pants and smiled weakly. After a few minutes of conversation, he went to the garage to work on his truck He got a phone call at four-thirty, and Emily called him inside to use her office phone.

"What would you like for dinner?" she asked.

"Whatever you'd like." He smiled at her and kept talking on the phone.

She winked back and left the office. In a few minutes, she called him on the intercom. "I'm going to the corner store for milk and bread. I'll be right back."

Roger opened the office window. "I'll go, Em."

"You don't have to do that—I don't mind." She waved him back inside, got in her car and drove off.

Roger felt panic rising. "I hope she doesn't notice that car," he said to Lady, but suspected she would. Emily was very perceptive, especially concerning safety. There were several burglaries in town that fall, and one occurred at a friend's house during the day while they were at work. Emily wanted to start a neighborhood watch. It was a good idea, except that most of the neighbors weren't within watching distance of each other.

Emily came back in a few minutes and walked directly into the house. Roger came in from the garage at five-thirty. She didn't mention the blue car.

Emily cooked a chicken dish they both enjoyed, and Roger forgot about the car. After the dishes were done, they sat in the living room watched a rented movie. He made a fire in the fireplace and poured wine. They munched popcorn and enjoyed the cozy, warm room.

Halfway through the movie, just as Roger was able to relax, the phone rang. Before he could move, Emily got up. "It's probably for me," she said. "Can you stop the movie for a minute?"

Although he wanted to disagree, he couldn't think of a good reason. He watched as she lifted the receiver.

"Hello? Yes. I called around five o'clock. It's about a quarter of a mile from here, parked alongside the road. It's a small blue car—I don't know the make, but it's a compact of some kind."

Roger's eyes widened. He stiffened, holding his breath. Emily had seen the car—even worse, she already reported it to the police!

"Sure. Feel free to call anytime. We're glad to help. Could you let us know whose it is when you find out? We're a little curious. Thanks a lot." She hung up.

"What was that about?" He tried to sound uninterested.

"Haven't you noticed that blue car parked by the road?"

"Car? What car?"

She studied him. "A little dark-blue car. It's been there for a while—there's still snow under it. I'm sure it was there yesterday when I got home. I reported it to the police. That call was Detective Hayes from the state police. They'll check the car, so I asked them to let us know who it belongs to."

Roger grimaced.

"You want to know who the car belongs to, don't you?"

"Oh, sure. We don't want burglars, do we?"

"What do you mean? It's a strange car parked a quarter mile from our house. It's been there for at least two days, and it might be stolen. Maybe it was a teenager on a joy ride or a rapist or murderer. Maybe it was *just* a burglar!"

"I'm sorry. I didn't mean to offend you. I just wish you told me before calling the police. One of our neighbors may've had car trouble, and he'll come back only to find his car missing. Do you want to be the one to tell him you called the police and they towed it away?"

Her glare softened a little. Roger stood up and put his arms around her, then he handed her a wine glass. "Come on. Let's not fight over a stupid abandoned car. Sit down. We'll finish the movie."

She looked at him. He'd been acting odd lately. "Do you know anything about that car?"

"Of course not! What makes you ask?"

She sighed. They watched the movie, and Emily seemed to forget the episode.

Roger couldn't. It preyed on his mind. He tried not to feel angry toward Emily, but he resented her actions. She didn't know, but he still felt betrayed. *Why didn't she tell me before she called the police?*

He slept poorly that night. Sometime around three o'clock, he finally slept deeply, only to be awakened by a nightmare.

"No! Please! NO!"

Emily shook him. "Wake up! You're having a bad dream."

Roger was drenched with perspiration.

"What was it?"

Lady got up and rested her head on the foot of the bed, her big brown eyes seeming to repeat Emily's question.

Roger felt physically and mentally exhausted, as if he'd not slept for weeks. Three days, it'd only been three days since the terrible incident. He hoped Emily wouldn't notice he was shaking.

She put her arms around him. "What is it, Roger? What's wrong?"

"It was just a bad dream. I dreamed a stranger tried to shoot me."

"That's terrible. Why? How?"

"I can't remember. It's...foggy." He did remember every cold and frightening detail.

"Can I get you something?"

"Water," he said, hoarsely.

She went into the bathroom and returned with a glass of water. Roger gulped it down and lay back on the pillow.

Emily got back into bed. They lay side-by-side in silence, then she said, "It was the wine."

"What?" He felt irritated.

"The wine. We shouldn't have had wine so late at night. You probably got indigestion, and that caused your bad dream."

"Oh. Maybe you're right."

The next day, Saturday, was bright and sunny. They got up at six and jogged two miles together, then showered when they got home. Neither mentioned the abandoned car still parked by the road. Emily felt the police would take care of it, and Roger didn't intend to mention the subject again.

He wanted to study the things he took from Gustafson's body, and waited impatiently for his chance. He was resigned to waiting until his terrible deed was discovered, then he'd surrender and hope for mercy.

As they sat in the kitchen eating muffins and coffee, Lady barked loudly.

"Who could that be at this hour?" Roger looked up at the clock which showed nine o'clock.

When he looked out the front window and saw a state police car pulling up, his heart skipped a beat. He gulped and leaned against a nearby chair.

Emily came to look. "I wonder if they've got more questions about that car?" She was calm.

Way to go, Emily, Roger thought. *They want your husband. They've come to drag me off to jail. Thanks a lot*!

Humphrey Brown

Three

Lady barked when the officer knocked at the door. Roger gulped, then opened the door. "Good morning, Officer. Please. Come in."

He wondered if the officer had a search warrant and would have come in, anyway. He wondered if his guilt showed on his face as much as he felt it did. Since there was only one officer, perhaps he wasn't there to arrest him. He tried to breathe slowly.

"Thank you. I'm Detective Hayes. I'm following up on a report of a blue car abandoned by the road. Is Mrs. Handley home?"

Roger cleared his throat, but before he could answer, Emily stepped forward.

"Oh, yes," she said. "I'm the one who called. I'm Emily Handley. It's nice to meet you, Detective Hayes. Did you find out who it belongs to?"

"It's a rented car, but we haven't been able to locate the person who rented it from an agency in Boston. Have either of you seen anyone unusual around here in the past few days?"

Roger and Emily both shook their head.

Detective Hayes was in his late thirties and had premature salt-and-pepper hair. He was polite, but deliberate. "It appears to have been rented on Monday and was due back yesterday. We checked the driver's license number given to the rental agency and couldn't find any record of it. It was probably a forgery."

Roger became interested. "What does that mean? Was he some kind of crook?"

Detective Hayes chuckled. "Nothing so dramatic. Most likely, it was a rendezvous, maybe with a friend or someone nearby, that didn't turn out well."

You got that right, Roger thought, *only it wasn't no friendly encounter*. "Got any leads?"

"Not really. We're just following up. Since you folks saw the car first, we wondered if either of you have seen or heard anything unusual."

"I haven't," Emily said.

"Me, neither," Roger shrugged and glanced at the floor.

"The rental company's sending someone over to pick up the car."

"Were there any clues in the car?" Roger asked.

The detective studied him for a moment. "Not even a glove or a road map."

"Isn't that odd, since it was rented in Boston? Wouldn't the driver need a map of the area?"

"Yes, it is, but it was a rental car. The person probably knew the area and didn't need a map."

"What rental company did he rent it from?" Roger couldn't stop himself from asking questions, even though something inside told him to cool it.

Detective Hayes considered his answer. "A Boston chain, but the company has a branch in Manchester, NH, and that's the office that'll come for the car." He paused. "What makes you think it was a man who rented it?"

Roger flushed and wanted to kick himself. "I don't know. I just assumed it. It could've been a woman. It was just a figure of speech. I thought you said it was a man."

Detective Hayes studied Roger, who tried to ignore the man's stare.

Roger shifted his weight awkwardly. "If there's anything…I mean, if we think of anything else, we'll let you know," Roger finished.

"Detective Hayes," Emily asked, "do you mind if I ask a question? There have been several burglaries in the area lately. Is there anything we should be aware of?"

"I know it seems like a lot," he answered, "but there have been only two reported burglaries in this town in the past three months. There's no reason to become alarmed. If you notice anyone who seems suspicious, please call the police. I doubt there's any reason to link that car with those break-ins. It's possible, but it's unlikely."

Emily nodded gratefully.

"There's no apparent explanation for the car yet," Detective Hayes continued, "but I intend to find out what it's all about. You can be sure of that." He glanced at Roger.

The officer started out the door, then turned back to give Roger a card. "If you notice anything suspicious, or remember something you overlooked, call me."

"We will." Roger gingerly accepted the card.

Detective Hayes paused, watching Roger for a moment, then he smiled at Emily and left. They watched him drive away.

"I hope they figure it out," Emily said.

"I'm sure they will."

"You seemed a little nervous. I never thought a policeman would make you nervous."

"He didn't make me nervous. What makes you say that?"

"You blushed." She just wanted to tease Roger, be he wasn't amused. She regarded him intently. "Is there something wrong? You've been acting strange lately."

"Come on, Emily. Don't make something out of nothing."

Emily thought about the nightmares, the dirty clothes, the distant look in Roger's eyes, and how he had trouble concentrating lately. She knew something was bothering him, but she didn't press it. She knew when to back off. Whatever it was, he'd work it out. She doubted it had anything to do with that blue car—it was probably just the pressure of trying to find work. She was sorry she had teased him. The last thing she intended was to add to his stress.

Roger showered and dressed, then went out for the paper and mail. He felt relieved when he saw the wrecker hooking up to the abandoned car to tow it away. It would be gone by the time George and Helen arrived. He didn't want any more questions.

George and Helen arrived exactly at noon. They got out of their car and Lady greeted them with excitement, her tail wagging.

George was a small man who preferred gourmet cooking to watching a football game, but could do both easily. Helen, his long-time companion, was equally petite. The gypsy in her showed in her manner and dress.

Emily hurried to finish the last minute lunch preparations as the couple came inside. "Hi, George!" She hugged her brother, then turned to hug Helen. "How are you two doing?"

"Great," George said. "Where's Roger?"

"He'll be right back. He just went out for some milk and a newspaper. Take your coats off and relax. Lunch is almost ready."

Roger arrived and everyone exchanged greetings. George was a friendly, huggable man. Roger was more reserved and found such behavior amusing, but he wasn't offended. He always hugged back.

Helen was affectionate, too. Roger assumed that was where George learned the habit. She hugged everyone—it was almost annoying.

They ate lunch and caught up on news. It'd been several months since George and Helen last visited. The last time was in August, when they went to Maine to stay for their annual week at Roger and Emily's cottage. They fished, sailed, swam, and had barbecues. The highlight was steak and lobster—turf and surf, they joked. They reminisced about their good time and laughed.

Roger was glad for the distraction. He and George talked about the recent Super Bowl, while Emily and Helen discussed the family, catching up on the latest gossip.

George and Helen were companions for years without getting married. Roger never inquired, but he often wondered why. Both were previously married, but it was a long time ago. Their marriages hadn't turned out well so he figured they must be more comfortable being officially uncommitted. Still, they behaved like a couple and sometimes they got testy and irritated with each other, which Roger usually found amusing.

Helen was irked when George interrupted her while she talked, something he often did. When she snapped at him, he said, "What? I thought you were done."

Emily caught Roger's eye when it happened, and they shared a grin.

The afternoon was spent talking. In the evening, Roger built a fire in the fireplace, and they sat with glasses of wine, chatting some more as the flames snapped and flickered, the stereo softly serenading in the background.

Helen considered herself psychic and often delved into New Age ideas. Emily eventually asked, "Helen, what have your psychic interests been lately? Anything new?"

"You won't believe this, but I can contact the dead!" She grinned. "Right now would be a good time. Want to try it?" She hoped they would say yes. "I'm sure to get something interesting."

Emily was always amused by Helen's antics. Roger laughed, and George made a face.

"Not again." George rolled his eyes. "You shouldn't encourage her."

Helen sat in front of the fireplace with her legs crossed and her hands palm up on her knees. She gazed into the fire and let the flames entrance her. Everyone waited silently, wondering what would happen.

After a few minutes, Helen started breathing more deeply, and she swayed from side-to-side. "I feel something," she whispered.

They leaned closer as Helen whispered and swayed.

"Ohhh. It's so dark, so cold…."

"What did she say?" George asked.

"Shhh!" Emily said.

Lady whined and got on the couch between Roger and Emily. Roger patted her gently.

"I feel sadness," Helen moaned. "Loneliness… Someone's crying for her loved one…" Her eyes were closed.

"What does that mean?" Emily whispered to Roger.

George made a face again, but Roger listened.

"There's someone here." Helen stopped swaying. "I feel an unfriendly presence. It's dark, cold, and evil."

"This is frightening!" Emily whispered.

"Oh, right," George said. "Real frightening. Be careful, or the bogeyman will get you."

"Don't be so skeptical," Emily said.

"Shhh, you two," Roger said. "She's saying something else." He was captivated by Helen's show.

"I hear a woman crying." Helen swayed again. "She's looking for someone. She's sad and lonely. There's nothing but darkness and cold. So sad…Crying…"

Roger felt nervous. *It couldn't be related to Gustafson's body in the well, could it?* he wondered. *Absurd. How could she know?*

"Ohhh!" Helen slumped forward.

"Too much wine, Helen?" George helped her to a chair.

She seemed disoriented.

"I told you not to encourage her," George said.

"Are you OK?" Emily asked.

"I guess so. What happened?"

"Don't you remember? You said you felt darkness, crying, and sadness."

George rolled his eyes. "Stop encouraging her, Em. She doesn't need it."

Emily glanced him a frown. He turned to Roger to discuss something else. Soon, they were engrossed in conversation. Roger glanced at the women, who went into the kitchen for tea.

Later that night, after George and Helen were settled in the guest room, and Roger and Emily went upstairs to bed, Emily asked, "What do you make of Helen's seance?"

"She's got one vivid imagination. That's all."

Emily was intrigued. "What if she really tuned into something? It sounded like someone was missing. Wouldn't it be amazing if she turned out to really be psychic?"

"Get real, Em. Helen's no more psychic than I am. You heard George. He knows her better than we do, and he thinks she's nuts."

"Roger, how can you talk like that? That's not like you. I never heard you be so derogatory toward my family."

He tried to repair the damage. "I didn't mean it that way. I just don't want you going off the deep end. It's not healthy. Look at Helen—she's out of touch with reality."

Emily thought about that. "You're right. It's too bad everyone isn't as wise as you." She tilted her head and looked him in the eye.

He smiled and put his arm around her. "You know me too well. You're right. I'm sorry."

The next day was bright and sunny. After breakfast, Roger and George repaired a small problem with George's car. Roger worked, while George watched.

A light dusting of snow fell during the night, and Emily and Helen decided to take a walk before lunch. But first, Emily came to the garage. "Roger, will you go to the store for me? I need a few things."

"Sure. What do you need?"

"I need three things. How about I make you a list?"

"What are they?"

"Green peppers, vanilla ice cream, and mayonnaise."

"No Problem. Don't write it down. I can remember that." He jumped into his truck and drove off.

At the store, Roger hurried down the aisles for the three items. He put peppers into the small basket he carried, then he chose his favorite brand of vanilla ice cream. Suddenly, he couldn't remember the third item.

He walked around the aisles, hoping he'd remember, but after ten minutes, gave up. He used the pay phone in front of the check-out counter to call home.

He fished a quarter from his pocket, studied the instructions, and dialed. The phone rang several times, and he was about to hang up when Emily answered, out of breath.

"I got the peppers and ice cream, but I can't remember the third thing," Roger said. "You sound winded."

"Roger, I had to run back to the house! You should have taken the list."

"What were you doing?"

"Helen and I want to explore the old well. She thinks the neighbor's cat, Mittens, got into it. Old Miss Timmons called right after you left to ask if we've seen her cat. It's been missing for a few days. We thought it might be in the well. Maybe that was what Helen got in her trance last night. The other item is mayonnaise."

"Don't go near that well!"

"Why not?"

"I...I don't think it's safe."

"Not safe? That's ridiculous. Don't be silly. We'll be careful. Don't worry. I have to run— Helen's waiting. Remember to get mayonnaise."

"Wait! Don't go. Emily?" No answer. **"Emily? Eimileee!"** All he heard was a dial tone.

Roger rummaged in his pocket for another quarter but didn't have any. He saw people staring, but he ignored them and ran to a nearby check-out counter.

"I need a quarter."

The clerk continued to ring up her customer.

"I need a quarter! This is an emergency!"

She looked at him. "I'm busy, Sir. I'll be with you as soon as I finish with this customer."

Outraged, Roger looked at the next clerk. By then, the manager was coming toward him.

"What seems to be the trouble, Sir?"

Too much time was passing. Roger left his items on the counter and ran out to his truck. As he sped home, he prayed he got there before Emily reached the well. He raced madly down the bumpy roads, wondering why the distance home suddenly seemed twice as long as it usually was.

Emily and Helen headed into the woods, scouting for the well. They were excited, thinking they may've experienced something extraordinary. Lady followed eagerly at their heels.

Roger raced down the road, fifty, sixty, seventy miles per hour. He kept looking around for policemen—no time to be stopped now—but he didn't see any.

Finally, he reached his driveway and drove down it like a madman. His truck slid to a stop, and he jumped out.

George was finishing something in the garage. He wiped his hands on a rag and looked up at Roger.

Where are the women?" Roger demanded.

"They took a walk. What's wrong?"

"Where?"

George pointed.

Emily and Helen struggled to remove the cover on the well. It had several broken spots where a small animal could easily fall through. When they pushed it aside, they peered into the darkness, then their eyes widened, and they screamed.

Roger ran toward the sound with George right behind. He intercepted the women as they ran toward the house. He grabbed Emily around the waist.

"It's terrible!" Emily said.

"Awful," Helen added. "It's the worst thing I ever say."

Roger released Emily and tried to calm them. "It's OK. Don't worry. I'll call the police when we get back to the house." He resolved to end his torture.

George caught up. "What's going on?"

"Call the police?" Emily asked. "You can't call them about that."

"What? We have to."

They walked toward the house.

"Why would you call the police about a dead cat?" Helen asked. "Shouldn't we just tell Miss Timmons?"

Roger stopped. "You saw a cat?"

"What did you think we saw?"

"I don't know. You screamed, and I assumed it was something terrible."

"What's going on?" George demanded.

"It was Miss Timmons' cat, and it was mutilated," Emily said. "Some animal must've attacked it, the poor thing. It was gruesome."

Helen nodded distastefully. "It was disgusting. Probably climbed in there to die. Remind me not to be so psychic the next time."

"Roger, we left off the cover when we ran away," Emily said.

"I'll take care of it."

"Let me help," George said.

"That's OK. You'd better accompany Emily and Helen back to the house. I'll be back in a minute." He ran to the well and found Lady standing on her hind legs, sniffing over the edge, whining as she tried to reach the dead cat.

Roger looked in. If it hadn't been for the cat laying on the boots, the women would've seen the body.

"Get down, Lady!" He replaced the cover and felt thankful for his luck. Still, he sensed time was running out, and he had to do something.

When he got back to the house, Emily was standing beside his truck. "Where's the groceries?"

He stopped, the color draining from his face.

"You forgot them?"

"I must'a left them on the check-out counter," he stuttered.

Emily frowned, but before she could scold him, George came to his rescue. "I'll go with you this time, and make sure you don't forget."

George nudged past Emily. Roger got in the truck with George.

"Thanks." he said. "I don't know how I forgot."

"Don't worry. You've obviously got a lot on your mind. Sometimes we men got to stick together."

As Emily and Roger waved good-bye to George and Helen later that afternoon, Emily said, "I told you Helen tuned in to something. Miss Timmons was glad to know what happened to Mittens. She feared never knowing. So you see, Helen is psychic, after all!"

Roger sighed. "Maybe I'll listen more closely next time." He put his arms around Emily, glad they had their peace and quiet back. He still wanted to look at the things he took from the body and wondered when he'd get the chance.

Four

When Emily left for the afternoon two days later, Roger went to the basement to retrieve the wallet, beeper, and pouch. He wondered what happened to the gun that almost killed him.

It's got to be there, buried in the leaves, he thought. *I'll go back in the spring and find it with a rake.* There was enough snow on it to hide it for the rest of the winter.

He put the items on the dining room table and removed everything from the wallet. He examined the credit cards closely and saw all were new, but issued to different names. The driver's license photograph was definitely the man he shot, and his name was Brian Gustafson.

Roger looked at the velvet-suede pouch. It was such a deep blue it was almost black, and it was surprisingly heavy for such a small bag. There was something inside that felt like marbles.

He dumped out the contents and stared in shock at a pile of beautiful polished stones—all various hues of pink, yet uncut for jewelry.

"Wow!" His jaw fell open. He wondered what they were. They were several sizes, some faintly pink, while others were almost the color of rubies. He held each up to the light and looked at it before carefully slipping it back into the pouch. He counted twelve and guessed they were each two to three carats in size.

Maybe Gustafson was a jewel thief. He wondered if the man was hiding them somewhere in the woods when Roger came on him that day.

He opened the wallet to investigate further, and a key fell out with a clang. It was a flat key with a red circular end. The unusual size and shape indicated it wasn't a regular door key.

Roger picked up the beeper and touched the button. When he pressed replay, the same message flashed on the tiny screen: *Change of plans. 8:30 at my office. JJ.*

I wonder what that means? Maybe that explains what he was doing out in the woods, Roger thought.

He got a note pad and pencil from the kitchen drawer and copied the message. He tore off the sheet, folded it, and turned off the beeper.

Time passed quickly as Roger studied the objects on the table. When Lady started barking, he realized Emily was back. He quickly gathered up the things and replaced them in their hiding place in the basement. The note went into his wallet. He was coming back upstairs when Emily opened the front door.

Emily carried bags of groceries in from the car and set them on the kitchen counter.

"Any more in the car?" Roger asked.

"Yes, two."

He went to get them.

"Guess who I saw at the store?" Emily asked as she unpacked groceries and put them away.

"Who?"

"Roberta, Rick's mother." Rick was Tony's classmate in high school. They lived on another street, with the back of their property abutting Roger and Emily's land.

"Anything interesting?"

"No, but she got a laugh when I told her how you fell out of the tree last week. Her husband's a doctor."

"What did you tell her that for?" Roger was irritated.

"Don't be so upset. She asked how we enjoyed our freedom now that the children are grown, just like them. Their son's away from home, too. I told her you were a bigger kid than any child. You hid from the dog and fell out of a tree. You have to admit, it's amusing."

Roger wasn't amused later in the day when Roberta's husband came to the door. Emily was in her office, and Roger was just going out the front door when a large black Cadillac came down the driveway.

Roger didn't know the people too well. Although Tony spent time with Rick, Roger and Emily never socialized with Rick's parents.

Roger stood in the doorway as the man approached. Jon was abrupt and direct—not a very popular man in the neighborhood. He was also the county pathologist. Roger thought that was a gruesome occupation.

All Jon's clothes were black, which enhanced the gold on the expensive watch on his wrist and the large ring on his left hand.

"Roger, isn't it?" Jon was obviously trying to act friendly beyond his normal inclination.

"Right. You're Jon, aren't you?"

They shook hands.

"How's Rick doing at college?" Roger asked.

"Roberta told me you hurt yourself in the woods last week. What happened?" Jon ignored Roger's question, and his own inquiry sounded like something other than neighborly concern about his well-being.

Roger shifted uneasily. If was obvious Jon hadn't come over to discuss Roger playing with his dog. "It's nothing. I fell out of a tree when I was playing with Lady." He stood in the doorway. "Now you'll have to excuse me, I was just on my way out."

Jon's expression changed to one of impatience. "Is that so? Let me look at your wound to make sure it's healing all right."

Roger clenched his fists, but kept them at his side, holding back his urge to throw this unwelcome intruder out of his home. "It's fine. It's all healed. There's nothing to show."

"I was home last week and heard some noises in the woods out back. It sounded like gunfire."

Roger remembered his sensation at the time that someone was watching from the woods. He swallowed hard. "I don't know what you're talking about."

"I believe you've got something that belongs to me!"

Jon shouted the last sentence, and Roger was worried Emily might overhear him. At least they were out of direct sight of her office.

"I have not idea what you're talking about. You'd better go."

Jon eyed him. "Perhaps the police would like to know about your injury." He glared at Roger.

Roger returned his stare. "I fell out of a tree and cut my arm. It's fine now. If you want to make something out of that, go ahead. Perhaps they'd like to know why you're so interested." He reached for the remote phone and turned it on. "Want me to dial the police for you?"

Jon's face turned red. "You haven't heard the last from me, Handley!" He pointed at Roger, then stomped off toward his car. A moment later, he sped out of the driveway.

Roger took a deep breath. His heart was pounding and his palms were damp. He went to the back door and glanced around the corner. Emily was working at her desk. He could hear faint music and realized she had the radio turned on—masking their loud conversation.

He left on his errands, wondering what the implications were of Jon's visit. He couldn't help but notice the striking physical similarities between himself and Jon. Both men were the same size, both had beards and dark hair. *Did Gustafson mistake me for Jon?* he wondered.

Later that evening, Emily asked, "What did Roberta's husband want?"

"He was collecting for a charity. I gave him a little something." It was getting easier to lie. "What do you know about them?" Since Emily was involved in local school activities while their children were young, maybe she'd be able to provide some insight.

"They aren't very popular."

Roger nodded. "He didn't seem the friendly type."

"Jon's the county pathologist. He's a little weird, probably from working on corpses all the time." She thought for a moment. "Rick was Tony's friend in grade school, but they didn't have much in common as they got older."

"Rick Wilson, right?"

"Yeah. That was always confusing, because her name is different."

"What do you mean?"

"She was his mother, but she married Jon later. Jon's the stepfather."

"So she has a different name?"

"Yes. Her name's Roberta Jong."

Roger was startled. "His last name is Jong? I never knew that. It's called the Wilson Farm."

Emily giggled. "That's right—Jon Jong, but she calls him JJ."

Over the next few weeks, Roger and Emily's life returned almost to normal and, much to Roger's relief, Jon didn't come back.

Roger played detective in his spare time. He went to the library several times when he was running errands in Concord, and so far, Emily didn't notice he was gone longer than usual.

He found some books on jewels and from photographs of uncut stones, he thought the jewels might be uncut diamonds, except they were pink. Roger made a list, inventorying all the stones, outlining their size and estimating their value. If he were correct, they might be worth as much as three million dollars.

He found a reference book that listed jewelers who specialized in cutting and resetting stones and wrote down several names and addresses. One in Quebec caught his eye. He liked the idea of visiting a foreign country.

He kept the items in his basement hiding place, but he put the list of jewels and jewelers in his wallet.

One day in early February, when Roger came home from running errands, Smitty's pickup was parked in the driveway. He hurried into Emily's office and found Smitty talking to her.

"Roger, it's horrible!" she said.

"What?" Roger glanced at Smitty.

"Your neighbor, JJ," Smitty said, "was found dead this afternoon. It looks like suicide."

Roger was stunned. "You're kidding. Dead?"

Emily nodded. "It was just on the radio."

"I was driving by and saw the police cars," Smitty explained, "so I knew something was up. I turned on my scanner and heard the message. Then I called Paul, the volunteer medic in town, and he told me JJ was dead when he arrived. He'd been shot in the head. It looks like suicide, but I'm not so sure."

Roger wondered. *Who killed JJ if it wasn't suicide? Is there someone else involved in this, maybe looking for the diamonds right now?*

He looked at Smitty. "It's amazing how you found out so fast."

"There ain't much that gets past me in this town." Smitty winked that knowing-wink of his, with a grin and mischievous twinkle in his eyes. Roger wasn't comforted by that.

Shortly after Smitty left, Lady started barking as Detective Hayes arrived. Roger gulped and Emily looked concerned.

"I hope everything's OK," she said. "Could this be related to that car?"

Roger invited the detective into Emily's office. "Hello. What brings you here?"

Detective Hayes glanced around the office and smiled at Emily, who sat behind her desk. "I've got bad news, folks. There was a murder not far from here—it was Jon Jong, your neighbor."

"We heard."

Detective Hayes was surprised.

"It was already on the radio." She pointed to the shelf. "Smitty, our neighbor, was here and told us, too."

"Oh." He smiled at Emily, again.

Roger felt a twinge of jealousy. The detective was taller and had thick, dark-brown graying hair that enhanced his handsome face. He was at least ten years younger than Roger, and **he** was employed. Roger wondered if Emily noticed.

"Murdered?" Roger asked. "I thought it was suicide."

Detective Hayes looked up. "It looked like suicide, but we're almost positive it was murder."

"How do you know?"

"Mr. Jong was left-handed, and the wound was on the right side of his head. That's not a likely way to commit suicide."

"You came here to tell us that?" Roger asked.

"Yes, and to tell you something else."

Roger and Emily waited.

"Do you remember that car you reported a few weeks ago?"

Emily nodded.   Roger looked grave, anticipating the worst.

"We believe it was rented by someone Mr. Jong knew, a man who dealt with him."

Roger didn't like the way the detective was looking at them. "What do you mean? What kind of deals?"

"We're not sure, but, if it's the man we suspect, he's very dangerous."   Detective Hayes pulled out a photograph and handed it to Roger. "Do you recognize this man? Have you seen him around here?"

Roger looked at the photo and shook his head. "No, I don't," he lied.

Emily looked at it next. "I'm sure I never saw this man before. Who is he?"

"He uses several aliases, but his real name is Brian Gustafson. He's a thief and murderer wanted in connection with several robberies in New York. In the last one, two guards were killed."

"What makes you think he's linked to Jong's death?" Roger asked.

Detective Hayes frowned. "For one thing, his fingerprints were on the gun that killed Mr. Jong. We suspect he's the one who rented the car. We can't figure out why he left it by the road for so long or where he went. He could be anywhere. You'd better be careful."

He turned to Emily. "You were concerned when you called us initially. We're watching the neighborhood. If you see anything suspicious, call immediately. Don't try to do anything on your own. This man is extremely dangerous."

Emily swallowed hard. "Are we safe here? JJ was here only a few days ago, and it's hard to believe he's dead."

Roger cringed.

"He was here?" Detective Hayes raised an eyebrow.

"Yes. He was collecting for a charity, right, Roger?"

"That's right. He stopped in for a moment. I hadn't met him before."

Detective Hayes looked at Roger, then at Emily. "As long as you two are here together and use some caution, you should be safe. You're really isolated out here. Be aware of your surroundings. Try not to worry, but call us the moment you notice anything."

He shook Roger's hand and left, smiling politely at Emily as he turned. Roger felt a twinge of jealousy again, which kept him from taking the detective inside the house to confess. Since the dead man was a known criminal, Roger might be able to convince a jury he fired in self-defense. Would Detective Hayes believe him? No, he wouldn't risk it. He had to protect Emily and their relationship. Roger was too embarrassed to speak up.

Roger and Emily were silent for a minute after Hayes left.

"This is incredible," Emily said. "I can't believe this. I have to send Roberta a card. The poor woman. Her husband was murdered."

Roger looked at Emily and wondered if she was in danger, too. He was more confused than ever. He had someone's stolen diamonds and a dead man in his well. To make things worse, he *knew* it wasn't Gustafson who killed JJ.

Who else is out there? Roger wondered.

That evening, they listened to the local news about Jon's death.

"Police now report that Mr. Jong's death may've been murder, not suicide," the announcer said. "That has left the village in a state of shock."

The story included a picture of where Jon was found. Roger saw a workbench filled with neatly hung unusual tools.

"What's that?" He turned to Emily. "Would he bring home his pathology tools?"

"Oh, Roger," she laughed. "Those are his hobby tools. He was a gemologist. He made jewelry. He must've been killed in his workshop. Roberta once mentioned he almost lived out there at times."

"You're kidding!"

"Didn't you ever notice all the jewelry she wears?"

Roger hadn't, but things were starting to make sense. Gustafson was expecting Jon that day, probably to sell some of the stones. *But if that's true,* Roger thought, *why did Gustafson shoot at me so quickly? Did he mistake me for JJ? Maybe he feared I'd remember him and turn him in.*

The newscast also showed a picture of the murder weapon. Roger recognized it immediately.

That's the gun Gustafson had! Roger thought. *No wonder I couldn't find it. Who did? Was it JJ or someone who came to murder him later? Did someone see me when I killed Gustafson?*

Detective Hayes was right—all the evidence pointed to Gustafson being the murderer. Only Roger and the murderer knew the difference. Roger felt uneasy, wishing he had a way to dispose of the stones, or better yet, just return them to their rightful owner.

He went to the library again the next day and read through old newspapers from the major Eastern cities. He started with Boston, where Gustafson rented the car, and New York, the address on Gustafson's driver's license.

He found an article about a jewelry store robbery that occurred in early January, the one Detective Hayes had mentioned. Two guards were killed in the robbery, and many uncut diamonds were stolen. There was no description of the stolen merchandise, but Roger was almost positive the stones he had were uncut diamonds.

There were no clues identifying the culprits, either. The insurance company was a Boston-based firm. Roger added the name and phone number to the piece of paper in his wallet, along with the name of the store that was robbed. It was a large jewelry chain with outlets throughout New England.

Five

Roger wanted to return the stolen diamonds to their rightful owners, but he didn't know how to accomplish that anonymously. He decided he needed to call an expert to get advice.

When Emily left to get her mail, he called Mr. LaBonte in Quebec, the jeweler on his list. She'd be gone for at least half an hour.

Roger picked up the receiver, then put it back down, then picked it up again, taking a deep breath. As he dialed, he wondered what he'd say. The phone rang several times, and he was about to hang up.

"Bonjour." It was a woman's voice.

"Hello?"

"Wait one moment. I'll get someone who speaks good English."

A few minutes passed, and Roger had second thoughts. He tapped his fingers on the table, glancing around the yard from the window. Finally, a man said, "Hello? Who is this?"

Roger cleared his throat. He hadn't planned on giving a name. "Hello, uh, this is…uh…Jack Smith. Um, are you Mr. LaBonte?"

"Oui. This is he. How may I help you?" The man sounded like he was in a hurry.

Roger gulped. He initially thought it would be easy to call someone and ask what to do with stolen uncut diamonds. "I have an uncut jewel, Mr. LaBonte, and I was wondering what to do with it. I understand you work with such jewels and thought you might be able to help me." He grimaced as he heard how weak he sounded.

There was a long silence. Roger regretted making the call and fought the urge to hang up.

"Mr. Smith, where did you get this jewel of yours, and what kind is it?"

"I got it from a friend. It's a diamond—I think. It's pink and about three to four carats." He blurted it out quickly.

"Pink?"

"Yes. Does that mean it's flawed?"

"Certainly not, Monsieur Smith. I would need to see the stone to evaluate it. I can't tell you much over the phone. If what you say is true, it could be cut and set. That would take a few weeks and I'd need to negotiate with you in person. Why don't you bring the jewel here?"

Roger sighed and cleared his throat again. "Mr. LaBonte, I need some serious advice, and I don't know where to turn."

LaBonte sounded like a direct but understanding man and since he didn't know Roger, he couldn't trace him. Roger blurted, "I found a pouch of uncut diamonds of many different sizes. They're all different shades of pink."

"You found them? They're all pink?"

"Yes. I don't know what to do with them. I suspect they were stolen from a New York store a few months ago, but there's no way I can return them without bringing suspicion on myself." Roger paused to catch his breath. It felt so good to tell someone, but he kept his finger on the button to hang up if LaBonte started acting odd.

They talked for fifteen minutes. Roger watched the clock above the window in Emily's office, keenly aware she'd be back soon.

Roger's evaluation of Mr. LaBonte seemed accurate. He was understanding and didn't ask too many questions. If Roger brought the stones to Quebec, Mr. LaBonte would discreetly return them to their rightful owner without Roger being implicated. Of course, he, Mr. LaBonte, would claim any reward offered for his troubles.

Roger agreed. He'd be happy to get rid of the gems as soon as possible and promised to call once he could make arrangements to bring the jewels to Canada, but that would be a while.

"I will forward you a copy of the return form from the insurance company," Mr. LaBonte said. "I've done this kind of thing before. Usually, someone steals something and becomes frightened and wants to return the item without being discovered. Other times, the stolen merchandise comes from unsuspecting customers who turn them in once they know the truth."

Roger assumed that meant Mr. LaBonte didn't deal in stolen merchandise.

Lady barked, and Roger realized Emily was returning. He said a quick thank-you and good-bye and hung up.

He thought a lot about Mr. LaBonte that day. The man sounded helpful, but what if he tried to trick Roger and kept the stones for himself? Worse, what if he turned Roger in?

Still, it would be so good to be free of the stolen jewels, Roger wondered if it might not be best to trust Mr. LaBonte after all.

That weekend, their son, Tony, and their daughter, Janet, came home to visit. It was the first time Roger and Emily saw their children since Christmas. Emily was consumed with preparations and anticipation for two days beforehand.

Tony arrived late Friday night, and Janet arrived Saturday morning. Saturday evening, Roger smoked his pipe after lighting a fire in the fireplace. The family enjoyed dinner together, laughing and catching up on each other's lives. Roger and Emily smiled as they listened to their grown children.

Tony sat opposite Roger in the living room, while Emily and Janet cleaned up in the kitchen.

"So, Dad, what's new around here?" Tony asked. "Did you ever get that buck?"

"No. Not this year." Roger puffed on his pipe, and the aroma of Captain's Blend filled the room.

"Did another hunter get him?"

"I don't think so. He's still around."

"I wish I'd been here. Maybe I can go with you next year."

Roger sighed. "I'm not sure I'll go hunting again next year."

"What? I don't believe it." Emily stood behind the sofa, drying her hands on a dish towel. Janet stood beside her.

Roger looked up without speaking.

"Yeah, Dad," Janet said. "You were obsessed with that buck. Why wouldn't you want to go after him again?"

Roger wished he'd answered Tony differently. "I'll just wait and see. I spent a lot of time hunting this year with nothing to show for it. Sometimes, it seems like a waste of time." He puffed on his pipe.

"I know your father," Emily said. "He'll be out there on the first day of hunting season. You can bet on it." She patted him on the shoulder, remembering the early mornings when Roger went out into the cold. She couldn't imagine him giving up something he obviously enjoyed so much. "He's just discouraged, that's all."

Roger realized he couldn't face the disappointment of his family if they knew what he'd done. Before contacting Mr. LaBonte, or taking any other action, he'd wait and let things calm down.

To his relief, nothing more had happened since JJ's death, and he hoped the worst was over.

Tony and Janet left Sunday afternoon. Roger and Emily hugged them as they got into their cars.

"When will you come home again?" she asked, wiping a tear off her cheek.

They assured her they'd be back as soon as they could. She understood they were grown, with their own lives to live, so she forced a smile and stood beside Roger as they waved good-bye. She leaned against him for a moment, then they walked into the house.

Emily was quiet as she always was after the children visited. Roger put his arm around her as they sat on the couch. "Let's see if there's anything good on TV," he suggested, hoping she'd cheer up.

As he scanned the channels, he stopped at a familiar program—America's Most Wanted. There was a photo of Gustafson in one of the segments. "Look at that!"

He turned up the sound and both he and Emily watched intently. "This man is considered armed and extremely dangerous," the announcer said. "Do not approach him. If you see him, call our toll-free number or contact your local police. He's wanted for the murder of two armed guards in New York."

"My God, Roger. That's the man Detective Hayes showed us. He's gruesome!"

Roger nodded as he watched in amazement. *So it was Gustafson who stole the jewels.* Roger felt his guilt ease a bit. At least the man he'd shot was a murderer. *But what connection did he have with JJ?*

April approached. Spring filled the air and Roger decided he'd soon be able to rent a tractor to fill in the old well, burying Gustafson and the nightmare forever. He thought he might as well toss everything he took from the body into the well, too, and be done with the whole thing.

Emily planned to spend the day spring cleaning, so Roger picked up the mail and used her office during the morning to plan some spring projects. Work might pick up soon and he was feeling better about his prospects.

At noon, Emily brought him lunch in the office and sat down to eat with him. She checked the mail as she ate her sandwich.

"Just bills," Roger said.

Emily nodded. "It looks like it." She opened the envelopes with her favorite letter opener and glanced at the contents.

"Thanks for the lunch," Roger said, as he ate the last of his sandwich. "I didn't realize I was so hungry."

"Would you like another sandwich?"

"No, thanks."

"Roger, this phone bill's a little high," Emily said, studying the statement. "Look. There's a mistake. We've got a call for Quebec listed."

Roger felt a pang in his gut, but he didn't look up. Emily frowned and reached into her pocket to pull out a small note she'd found in Roger's clothes when she did the laundry that morning. Roger ignored her and hoped she'd look at the next piece of mail.

"Who do you know in Quebec?" she asked.

"No one." He still didn't look up.

"Roger."

He glanced at her and saw the note in her hand. His face turned red.

"This is yours, isn't it? It's the same number as the one on our phone bill. You must've called someone. Don't you remember who you called?" She studied him intently. It wasn't the amount of money that bothered her, it was the feeling he'd lied. She was hurt and couldn't understand why he'd do that.

"Oh, yes. I forgot." He squirmed in his chair.

Emily waited for a further explanation, thinking, *this better to be good*. Roger hesitated so she reached for the telephone. "Maybe I should call and find out who it is."

"No! Emily, don't do that. It was something about a possible job. I didn't tell you, because I didn't want you to be disappointed if I didn't get it. That's all."

She looked at him, then she looked at the envelopes on her desk and shoved them into her drawer. She walked back into the house without speaking.

As soon as she left, Roger opened the desk drawer, but the note wasn't there. He hurried into the house and found Emily using the phone. She glanced at him, her expression grim, then she turned away.

"Who are you calling?"

She gazed out the window and didn't answer. Finally, she heard a voice speaking French. "Can you speak English? Good. I need to know who I've reached. Mr. LaBonte? Yes, I would. I can wait."

Roger walked over and pushed down the button on the telephone. "It was just a wrong number, Emily."

Her eyes filled with tears. She pulled out the telephone bill from her pocket. "You never lied to me before, Roger—at least, not that I know of. Since when does a wrong number last twenty-three minutes?"

Roger's jaw dropped. He was speechless. Never before had he felt so guilty. He realized she'd been suspicious of him ever since that terrible day in January, and that he'd been deceiving her all along, believing it was to protect her. Now he knew he was only fooling himself.

He faced a dreadful choice. He could keep lying and destroy his trust with her, or he could confess and risk losing her forever. One thing he knew for sure, if he told the truth, she'd never think of him the same way again.

Roger sat down. A large tear rolled down his cheek. "I'm so sorry, Emily. I really am."

She was surprised and frightened. Whatever Roger's secret was, it was bigger and more powerful than she'd suspected. Yes, indeed she'd noticed the change in him over the past few months, but assumed it was due to the recession and his lack of work. She dismissed his moods as depression, assuming he would improve when work picked up again.

Emily put her arms around his shaking shoulders and tried to comfort him. Suddenly, all the fear from that first moment in the woods when Gustafson shot at him, through the visits by the police, and the questions about the abandoned care, all came flooding back.

He cried bitterly. Emily held him, her anger replaced by compassion and fear. Whatever was wrong, she loved him and would stand by him.

"What is it, Roger? Please tell me."

He slowly regained his composure. When he looked at her, he saw tears on her cheeks, too. He felt closer to her than ever before and realized how strong their love was.

"I'm sorry I deceived you. You must believe I only wanted to protect you." His voice broke and he took a deep breath to start over. "I did something terrible!"

Emily waited quietly.

"Back in January, shortly after hunting season ended, while you were away for the day, I...."

"Go on."

"It was the day you received your award, remember?"

She nodded.

"I decided to do something really stupid—I went hunting. I know it was out of season, but I really wanted that buck. I wanted you to be proud of me and respect me. I thought if I gave you the venison, you'd be happy."

He sighed. "I waited in my hunting stand for a few hours, but the buck never came. I heard something in the thicket, so I climbed down to investigate."

"When I did, I discovered a mean-looking man with a scar on his chin coming toward me." He stopped to gather his thoughts, which were coming at him so fast, he didn't want to get anything wrong.

"I panicked. I had my rifle, and I thought he was a game warden. I set my rifle behind a boulder. I knew the man saw me, so I pretended to be out walking. Then he shot me."

"Shot you? My God! Why?"

"I don't know. The first shot hit my knife and the second grazed my arm. That was the wound I had when I told you I'd fallen out of a tree."

"He shot you twice! You were hit? Oh, no, Roger! What did you do?"

"I ran back to the boulder and grabbed my rifle. I...I shot him, Em. I didn't mean to, but when I rolled over, my rifle went off almost by itself. I was so scared, I probably did it on purpose, but I'm not sure. It all happened to fast."

"Oh, Roger. Why didn't you tell me?"

"He was dead. I shot him right between the eyes."

They sat silently for a while. Roger worried that Emily wouldn't love him anymore, that he may've just lost everything in the world that meant anything to him.

Emily was shocked and wondered if the story was true. She looked at Roger's tired face and knew he was telling her the truth. "What did you do? Where's the dead man's body?" She wondered how she could sound so calm.

Roger was surprised by the lack of judgment in her voice. All he heard was concern. "I put the body in the old well, where you and Helen found the missing cat."

"You're kidding. You mean we almost discovered the body? No wonder you hurried home and tried to stop us."

Roger smiled weakly. "Em, the man I shot was Gustafson. Do you remember Detective Hayes telling us about him?"

"Oh, my god, Roger."

Emily sat thoughtfully for a moment. Roger wondered what else he could tell her. Then she said, "But how could Gustafson have murdered JJ if he was already dead?"

"I don't know." Roger frowned. "I've been trying to figure that out since it happened. It obviously wasn't Gustafson who murdered JJ, but it was definitely **his** gun. There has to be someone else involved."

"His gun?"

"Yes. I recognized it on the television news that night. I went back to the site in the woods a few days after I'd shot Gustafson, but I never found the gun he shot me with. I figured it was lost in the leaves and I'd be able to find it in the spring."

"You're sure it was his gun?"

"Yes."

"What does that mean?" Emily looked him squarely in the eye.

"It means someone else found the gun. It might have been JJ. That day he stopped by here, he said he'd heard shots in the woods. He might have heard Gustafson attack me."

"Is there anything else you're not telling me?"

"Wait here a minute." He went into the cellar and retrieved the things he took from Gustafson's body.

Emily walked over to the kitchen counter to see the things Roger had.

"I got these from his body," Roger explained. "Here's his New York driver's license. These credit cards all have different names, which are probably some of his aliases that Detective Hayes mentioned."

"What's that?" She pointed at the velvet pouch.

He dumped the contents onto the counter.

Emily gasped. "They're beautiful! Are these the ones that were stolen in New York?"

"I think so. My guess is Gustafson planned to meet someone in the woods that day, or else he planned to hide the gems there."

"They're gorgeous." Emily looked at them carefully. "What kind of jewels are they?"

"I think they're uncut diamonds."

"Pink diamonds? That's odd. I never saw a pink one." She thought about Roger's story. "What about JJ? Could Gustafson have been meeting him?"

Roger eyed her soberly. "If that's true, he may have mistaken me for JJ. We do look a lot alike."

"Did."

Roger frowned. "Did look a lot alike."

He sighed. "Perhaps he just didn't want me to witness their transaction."

Emily was startled. "He intended to murder you? You're sure?"

"**Very sure**."

Emily felt conflicting emotions. "Why didn't you tell me? I thought we never kept secrets from each other."

"I didn't want to implicate you. I was afraid you might be an accessory after the fact."

Emily sighed a reluctant acceptance of his statement. "Why would you go hunting out of season? Norman was right, you *did* go hunting that day." She shook her head and rolled her eyes.

"It was stupid. Please forgive me. I promise I'll never do anything like that again."

Emily sat thoughtfully for a moment. "You must've been really upset when I called the police about that blue car."

Roger nodded.

"I'm sorry. I didn't know," she said.

Roger smiled weakly. "It's probably for the best. By calling, Detective Hayes trusts you. He doesn't seem to like me too much, but he knows you as the one who reported Gustafson's car. It makes me, and us, look innocent. So, in a way, you did me a favor."

Emily sighed. "What about this call to Quebec?"

"I called a jeweler named LaBonte to ask him how to anonymously return the jewels to their owner. He said he'd help me if I brought him the jewels, but I'm not sure I'm comfortable with that. I don't know him. It might be a trap, or he might report me to the police, so I decided to hold off on that."

"Couldn't you just return them yourself?"

"How would I explain being in the woods with my gun out of season? Then I'd have to explain hiding the body in the well. I'm innocent, but I don't look it. What would happen to you—to your well-deserved standing in the community? Do you want everyone talking about us?"

"Couldn't you just say you found the pouch in the woods? Or along the side of the road or something?"

"Then I'd look even more guilty. Don't forget, they know Gustafson's car was parked near here. If they ever discover his body hidden in our well, how do we explain that? It'd be too risky."

Emily nodded. No wonder Roger was acting so oddly, she thought. He was in a dilemma, and she wanted to help. "We have to go to the police. I'm not worried about my community standing, Roger. I'm worried about you, and us. Let's call Detective Hayes and explain all this to him."

"No way! That's final!"

"Then what can we do?"

"I don't know, but time's on our side. The longer we wait, the better. Time may distance the whole affair and maybe things will die down and go away. It's been a month since JJ's murder."

"What'll happen if someone finds Gustafson's body in the well? You said yourself, it could happen."

"They won't. I'm going to fill it in as soon as the ground dries out enough to bring in a tractor. Even if they do find the body, without the diamonds, they won't connect him to me." He looked into her eyes. "You can't tell anyone, Emily. Promise me you won't."

She hesitated. "I won't." She understood, it was a problem he needed to resolve, and she had no intention of telling anyone.

During the rest of the day, they discussed the incident and tried to figure it out. Both were exhausted and emotionally drained when they went to bed that night. Even though she was tired, she kept thinking about the beautiful pink jewels.

For the first time in months, Roger fell asleep. His soul felt cleansed, and Emily still loved him.

Despite her promise to Roger, Emily slowly formulated a plan of her own. She would put it into action the next day.

Humphrey Brown

Six

Emily slipped on her sunglasses as she left the house the next day, not because of the bright sun light on the snow, but because it fit her clandestine mood and intentions. Even after she entered the quaint shop in downtown Concord, she left her glasses on.

It was nearly six o'clock, and she knew the shop would soon be closing for the day. She browsed around the back aisles, waiting for the other customers to leave. Alex, the owner, was ready to lock the door when he noticed her.

"I'm sorry, Ma'am, but we're closing."

Emily removed her sunglasses and smiled at her old friend.

"Emily! How nice to see you. It's been too long—almost three years."

Alex was as eccentric as the items he sold in his shop. It was renowned as the best place in the area to find special and unique presents. Emily worked with him many years ago, when her children were young, before becoming an accountant. He liked the jute wine racks she made and sold exclusively in his store.

Except for whiter gray hair and a little more stoop to his shoulders, Alex looked the same. He wore the same kind of sweater, gray wool, and it was unbuttoned enough to show the suspenders holding up his wide-legged trousers.

His half-lens glasses slipped down his nose, allowing him to look over the top with his kind eyes. Everyone liked Alex. He was a fixture in the town.

Over the years, Alex became more than a client of Emily's. He was one of the first to encourage her when she returned to college for her degree. Even though he'd miss her wine racks, he congratulated her when she became a Certified Public Accountant, and he was her first client, until his own son became an accountant, too.

She felt she could trust Alex. He knew a lot about unusual items. She touched the gem wrapped in a tissue in her pocket.

"Hi, Alex. I'm sorry to keep you so late."

They hugged.

"Nonsense. I'm glad to see you. How have you been?"

"I have a problem. I hope you can help me." She spoke quietly, as if fearing someone might overhear.

Alex patted her arm affectionately. "Wait here. I'll close the shop, and we can talk in my office."

Emily nodded and stood near the back door that led to the storage area and Alex's office. It brought back memories of years ago when she'd come there to deliver her goods, small children in tow. He'd always been so helpful.

Alex locked his front door, reversed the OPEN sign to CLOSED, and turned off all but one light. He walked back to Emily and led her into his office.

He motioned her into the only extra chair in the small room, then sat behind his neat desk and picked up a pencil. "What's the problem, Emily? How can I help?"

Emily hesitated. The previous night, it seemed logical to ask Alex to find out the best way to return the uncut jewels anonymously, but at the moment, she wondered if the story would sound so ridiculous even her good friend, Alex, might not believe it. Or might refuse to get involved. It suddenly occurred to her that she might be expecting too much, even for their good friendship.

"I need to know what to do," she began. "Someone I know very well has asked me for advice, and I'm not sure what to tell him."

"Go on," he encouraged, smiling over his glasses.

Emily blushed, adding to her embarrassment. She wished she hadn't come, but decided to continue carefully. "My friend has come across a group of diamonds that appear to be valuable and he has good reason to believe they're stolen."

"Stolen?" Alex's smile faded.

"He didn't steal them," she added quickly. "They came to him...by accident. How can he get the diamonds back to the rightful owners without implicating himself? Is that even possible?"

Alex sat silently, thinking hard. "Are you quite sure they're stolen?"

She nodded, shifting in the wooden chair which seemed uncomfortably hard.

"How do you know?"

"From several sources, including the police and the news reports."

He nodded. "Ok. They're definitely stolen. Do you have any idea where they came from?"

"A jewelry store in New York City."

Alex's eyebrows raised. "Really? Probably from the diamond district. That's interesting. This friend of yours wants to return them to the store, I take it?"

"Yes. To the store or whoever can get them to the store. It might be the police or perhaps the insurance company."

Alex sat thoughtfully for a moment. "I'm no jeweler, Emily. It's not my specialty."

Emily removed the tissue from her pocket and unwrapped the diamond. It had a beautiful light-pink hue as she held it under the lamp on the desk. Alex leaned forward to admire it.

"May I?" he asked.

"Sure." She handed him the uncut stone.

"I've never seen anything like this before. A pink diamond? I've heard of them—they're from Australia. And they're very rare and *very* valuable."

"Australia?"

Alex looked at her over his glasses. "That's what I've heard, but don't quote me. I'm no diamond expert."

Emily sighed, then frowned. "Can you help me? It's very important. Someone has already been murdered over these stones, and the person who has them wants very much to be rid of them."

"Murdered! Good Lord, Emily! Do the police know?"

"I don't know. I can't go to them. It's complicated and I can't explain it right now." She looked at him tearfully. "Can you help me?"

He sensed her despair and desperation, and smiled. "Don't worry. I might be able to help your...friend. It seems to me, the best approach would be to return them to the insurance company, which is probably hoping they'll turn up. Then they won't have to pay off the customer's claim. There's probably a reward offered, too."

"I, uh, that is we, I mean, my friend, doesn't care about any reward. They just want to remain anonymous."

"I see."

"Do you have any idea which insurance company it is?" Emily asked.

"No, but I've got a friend in the business, and I'll ask him who the biggest diamond insurer is. I'm confident I can find out. These aren't common stones. Can I keep this one until I see you next?"

Emily looked worried, not because she didn't trust Alex, but because she didn't want Roger to know one of the gems was missing. She'd only brought it in case Alex didn't believe her.

"I'll find a safe place to hide it, Emily. I may need to confirm my story just as you did." He looked at her over his glasses and tipped his head slightly to one side.

She bit her lip. "All right." She hoped she could return it before Roger noticed, after all, what were the chances he'd actually sit down and count the remaining stones?

Alex frowned. "Emily, I'm not trying to tell you your business, but you must be careful. If the police find out you're involved, even though you're just trying to help a friend, you might be in trouble, too. Have you thought about letting your friend solve this himself?"

"I understand." She fidgeted in her seat. "You won't say anything, will you?"

He eyed her for a long moment. "If anyone comes snooping around, I don't know anything." He raised his eyebrow. "I'll keep your secret, Emily, but you will have to do the same for me."

"Oh! I'd never mention your name to anyone, either, Alex. Be assured of that. I'll keep you out of it. I appreciate your help. Perhaps I shouldn't have come, but I didn't know where else to turn." She knew she was rambling and stopped herself with a shrug.

The awkward moment passed.

"How can I reach you?" Alex asked. "Is your phone number still the same? I've got it somewhere. Do you have a business card?"

Emily opened her purse and pulled out a baby-blue business card, then wrote her home phone number on the back. "You can reach me at either number, Alex, but, please, don't talk to anyone but me."

He stood up and pinned the card to his bulletin board, then turned back to her. "I'll unlock the door for you now. I'll call as soon as I have some information. Try not to worry, and tell your friend the same. I'm sure we can find some way to resolve this." He smiled at her.

Emily walked ahead of him to the front door, then turned around after he unlocked it. "Thanks, Alex. I appreciate this." She gave him a hug, and turned to leave.

She walked to her car. The sun was setting, so she didn't need her sunglasses anymore, but she put them on, anyway. Somehow, it felt safer.

She stopped at the grocery store on her way home, and Roger never suspected a thing.

Emily hadn't expected to hear from Alex right away, but he called before lunch the next day.

"Hi, Alex," Emily said, surprised. Roger was in the office at the time, looking for something. "Yes. That sounds good. Six o'clock tonight? Sure. I can be there. Really? I appreciate that,. Alex. I'll be there. Thanks."

Emily put the phone down and glanced at Roger. Suddenly, she felt guilty and wondered if she'd done the right thing. Alex did say he had the answers for her.

She was anxious to meet him and hoped she could help Roger. Still, something bothered her, but she couldn't quite recall it—it was something Alex said the previous night.

Emily spent the rest of the day waiting restlessly.

After five-thirty, Emily told Roger she had to go to town to meet a client.

"Who?" Roger remembered her mentioning six o'clock in her phone conversation earlier that day and wondered about it. Emily's work day was always kept separate from her private life, and she rarely made exceptions.

"Alex." She felt uncomfortable hiding things from Roger.

"Your old craft store friend?"

"Yes."

"A business meeting at this hour?"

"Yes." Emily stood at the door with her hand on the knob. "Why don't you come with me? You can drive."

She didn't know why she said that, but she secretly wanted Roger to come with her. She was worried after JJ's death and concerned that it was related to the stolen diamonds.

Roger thought for a moment. "All right. I need to get some beer. I'll go to the store while you're in your meeting and pick you up afterward. How's that?"

"Great. We'd better hurry. It's nearly six now, and we don't want to keep Alex waiting."

As they approached the center of downtown Concord, they saw flashing lights and cars parked in front of Alex's store. Emily watched, confused.

"Must be an accident." Roger said as he approached slowly, but he didn't see any wrecked cars. There were several police cars parked nearby, their lights flashing, and an ambulance was in the middle of the street. A policeman strung yellow ribbon across the front of Alex's store.

"Stop the car!" Emily said.

"What?"

"STOP!"

The car barely came to a stop before Emily jumped out.

"Emily, come back!"

She ran off without answering.

A policeman motioned to Roger to keep going. Roger looked for Emily, but she disappeared into the crowd in front of the shop.

The impatient policeman tapped Roger's window with his flashlight.

"Ok, I'm going." Roger shook his head. "Damn it. Emily. What are you doing?"

Roger parked as close as he could and hurried back to find Emily.

Emily went to the front of the crowd and stood against the yellow tape. Something had happened in Alex's shop. Then her eyes met those of Detective Hayes as he came out of the shop door. He blinked in surprise, then came toward her.

"What happened?" Emily asked. "Is Alex all right?"

Detective Hayes didn't answer, because the ambulance team came out just then with a body on a stretcher.

"Just a minute," he said.

He pulled down the sheet and let Emily see the man's face. It was Alex.

"Oh, my God!"

"You knew the deceased, Mrs. Handley?"

Emily nodded, in shock.

"Would you come with me?" He took her arm and escorted her into the store.

Roger walked up in time to see Emily and the detective disappear inside the building. "What happened?" he asked folks standing nearby.

"The store owner, Alex, was found dead," a woman in the crowd answered. "It looks like murder. They just brought out the body."

Roger looked inside the store window and saw Emily talking to Detective Hayes. "Oh no, Emily," he whispered, "what have you done?"

Inside the store, Emily felt a sense of deja vu. She'd been there the previous day to talk to her old friend, and the store looked the same.

"What happened to Alex?" A tear fell down her cheek.

"Come back here so we can talk." Detective Hayes motioned toward the storeroom beside Alex's office.

Then Emily noticed the diamond she'd left. As Alex promised, it was well-hidden—right out in the open. It sat in the middle of a white silk flower on a straw hat in the front window.

As the detective turned away, Emily snatched the diamond off the hat and put it into her pocket. Detective Hayes turned to see what was delaying her, and she smiled weakly, wondering if anyone saw her take the stone. Her heart beat rapidly, and her face flushed.

She walked toward Detective Hayes.

"I found this on his desk, Mrs. Handley." He showed her a page from Alex's calendar. It had her name written on it, along with the words, 6 p.m.

Emily noticed he wasn't referring to her as Emily anymore, but as Mrs. Handley. He wasn't as friendly as he'd been before.

"Mrs. Handley?"

She tried to think of an answer.

"You were a friend of the deceased? You were to meet him here at six o'clock tonight?"

Emily nodded. "That's why I'm here. We were supposed to meet after he closed the store." She looked around.

"Why?"

"Why?" She was confused.

"Why after he closed?"

"He is..was..a dear friend. I used to sell things in the store. He wanted to discuss me doing that again."

Detective Hayes liked Emily and thought perhaps she was acting so oddly from shock. "Is that all?"

"What?"

"Is that the only reason you came, to sell things in the store?" He jotted down notes on a piece of paper.

"Yes." She watched the policemen and women going in and out of Alex's office. "Is that where he...?"

"Yes. He died there."

"How?"

"He was murdered."

"Oh, God, no!" She reached for the wall and tried not to faint.

Detective Hayes went to the office door and whispered to the officers at work inside. They left. He motioned Emily to come over. "I know it's hard, but, since you're familiar with the place, could you take a look in here and see if anything's missing or out of place?"

"Do you think it was robbery?"

"We don't know. I'm hoping you might shed some light on that. Will you take a look. Take your time. It's messy, and well...take a look."

Emily reluctantly approached the door. She looked in. Her hand went to her mouth as she looked around the small office. The room was splattered with blood, the desk had been ransacked, and Alex's bulletin board was on the floor.

She glanced around in terror. She cried softly, and Detective Hayes began to have second thoughts about showing her the office. Slowly, she stepped inside.

She bent down toward the bulletin board, looking for her business card, but it wasn't there. She looked on the floor, too, but it wasn't anywhere.

"Did you take anything out of here?" she asked.

"No, just this calendar sheet, the body, and the knife."

"That's all?"

"Yes. Why? Is something missing?"

Emily sighed and stood up. "I don't know. I thought there were more papers on this bulletin board when I was here last night, but..."

"You were here last night?"

She blushed. "That's when I last saw Alex. He was anxious to work with me on my crafts." She wondered if he really believed she had time for such things as crafts being an accountant, and she looked around the room, unwilling to meet his eyes.

"I have to get out of here. I'm going to be sick." She ran toward the front of the store.

Detective Hayes followed her. She stopped at the cashier's bench and leaned on it, trying to regain her composure.

"Take your time, Mrs. Handley. I'm sorry to put you through that. I shouldn't have taken you in there. It's gruesome. Our problem is, we don't have many clues. Everyone knew Alex was harmless, and we can't figure out who'd want to kill him like that."

"He was the sweetest man I knew. I've known him for over twenty years, and I can't believe he's been murdered. How was he killed?" She looked into the detective's eyes.

"Slowly." He grimaced.

"He was tortured?"

The detective nodded grimly. "Whoever killed him wanted something."

Emily was so shocked by the last revelation, that she urgently wanted to get out of there. She reached into her pocket for a tissue to dry her eyes, and she accidentally pulled out the diamond, caught inside. She tried to hide it in her hand.

Detective Hayes reached for her hand and Emily didn't know what to do, so she put the tissue back in her pocket before taking his hand. "My tissue," she said, apologetically.

He nodded. "Here's my card, Mrs. Handley." He studied her briefly, making her even more self-conscious. "Where's your husband?"

Emily felt her body jolt with a start. "He's...He's out there somewhere, waiting for me. He dropped me off for my meeting with Alex."

"Has he been with you all day?"

"Yes."

He smiled slightly. She didn't feel any better.

"Please call if you think of anything that might help," he said.

"I will."

As she opened the door, Detective Hayes said, "Emily?"

She stopped and looked at him.

"It's an odd coincidence to have two people die near you, but don't worry. We'll find the killers."

Emily's eyes became wide. "Could the two murders be related?" She wanted to take back her words the moment she said them.

"Related?" He shrugged. "How? Could they have been committed by the same person?"

"I've got to go!" Emily said, and ran outside.

Roger saw her leave the store and pushed his way toward her through the crowd. She ducked under the police ribbon and sagged into his arms, crying softly.

"Let's get out of here," Roger said.

They hurried to the car. Emily cried hysterically for a few moments, her face in her hands. Roger tried to calm her.

"What is it, Emily? What happened? Was it Alex?"

She looked at him with tears falling down her cheeks, then pulled out the diamond and opened her hand. The light of the street lamp reflected on it through the car's window, enhancing the pink glow.

"Oh, God," Roger said. "What have you done?"

Seven

Roger realized Emily was too near hysteria to explain much, so he started the engine and backed out of his parking space. "Let's go home."

They drove towards their house in silence and Emily's crying gradually subsided. Suddenly, she said, "Stop the car."

Roger glanced at her in confusion.

"Stop the car, Roger. Right now!"

He pulled over.

"We can't go home." Her eyes were full of fear.

"What are you talking about?"

"It's not safe."

"What? Tell me what happened back there. Did you tell Alex about the diamonds? What is it, Em? Talk to me!"

She looked around. "Let's go someplace where we can talk—I feel pretty exposed out here."

Spooked by Emily's anxiety, Roger agreed. "Ok. How about if we go to Fred's Place."

She nodded.

Fred's Place was a popular diner on the outskirts of town. There were always lots of people there, and Roger and Emily found a booth. Being in a crowd made them feel safer.

Once they were seated, a waitress brought them a menu.

"Can we have a minute?" Roger asked.

The waitress noticed Emily's red eyes and nodded. "Take all the time you want." She walked off.

""What happened, Emily? You've really got me worried."

"Roger, it's terrible! Alex is dead. I can't believe it." She wiped her eyes with the napkin.

Roger sighed. "He was old, Emily. Maybe he had a heart attack." His statement almost sounded like a question.

"He was murdered." Tears filled her eyes again.

"Oh no, Emily! Who would do that? He was a harmless old man." It was no wonder Emily was shook up, but Roger wanted to hear more.

"Roger, I feel terrible. It's all my fault."

Alarm showed on his face. "What do you mean?"

Emily felt a mixture of grief, guilt, and anger and wondered how to explain herself. She'd betrayed Roger's confidence after promising not to tell anyone, and the consequence felt unbearable.

"Em, talk to me. What did you do?"

That was too much. "What did *I* do? I didn't get us into this mess. I didn't go hunting illegally and shoot someone!"

Roger glanced around in concern. "Keep it down, Emily. Do you want the world to know?"

Emily glared at him, but she forced herself to be quiet, holding back further comment.

The waitress came back. "Ready to order now, folks?" She glanced at them.

"We'll have two of your specials," Roger said.

Emily avoided eye contact with both of them as her mind sought an answer to what had happened.

As soon as the waitress left, Roger spoke kindly. "I'm sorry, Emily. I've made some stupid mistakes. I didn't mean to imply you did anything wrong."

Emily gave him a thin smile. "I know. I'm just upset."

"Tell me what happened. I need to know everything."

"I went to see Alex yesterday. I know you didn't want me to tell anyone…"

Roger groaned. "That's why I didn't want to tell you about this. Em, how could you?" He saw her angry look and calmed himself.

"I've known Alex for twenty years, Roger. I knew I could trust him and if he could, he'd help us, so I told him."

"Just what did you tell him?"

"I said I had a friend who found some stolen diamonds and who wanted to return them without getting implicated. That's all."

"Are you sure?"

"Yes. He told me he'd discreetly find out how to return the gems. He called this morning and told me to meet him at six tonight. He said he had some information for my friend."

Roger was not pleased, but he tried to make the best of the situation. Emily paused.

"Why was he murdered?" Roger asked.

"Detective Hayes showed me the office. There was blood all over the desk and floor. It was horrible. Alex was tortured." Her voice sank to a whisper.

Roger looked into her eyes. He saw perspiration on her brow. "Why did he show you the crime scene, Em? What does that detective know?"

"All he knows is that I was supposed to meet Alex at six." Her face flushed.

"Geez, Emily! He's got to be suspicious. First the car, then JJ, and now Alex! God, he must figure we're involved—that's just too much of a coincidence."

Emily understood Roger's concern, and deliberately omitted the question Detective Hayes had asked about his whereabouts that afternoon. "I don't think so, Roger. I told him I was meeting Alex to discuss business. He saw my name on Alex's calendar. When he saw me in the crowd, he thought I might be able to tell if something was missing from Alex's office. They probably suspect it was a robbery."

The waitress returned with their meals. Roger and Emily felt calmer. The hubbub of the restaurant helped distance them from Alex's death.

To his surprise, Roger was hungry. After chewing a big bite, he looked at Emily. "Why do you have that diamond in your pocket? Why were you worried about going home?"

Emily gulped. "I left the diamond with Alex last night, in case he needed proof."

Roger stopped eating and looked at her as she bit her lower lip. Instead of words, he rolled his fork to indicate, *and then what?*

"I retrieved it from his store when I saw where he'd hidden it," Emily continued. "I grabbed it when no one was looking." She looked meekly into his eyes.

She lowered her voice to a whisper. "I left my business card with Alex yesterday, and he pinned it to his bulletin board. I saw him do it, but it wasn't there when I was in his office with Detective Hayes."

"Maybe it fell down?"

"No, it didn't. I looked everywhere. It was gone."

"Did you tell the detective?"

"I didn't say a word." She took a small bite of food and chewed as if it were tasteless. She was no longer hungry and absentmindedly picked at her dinner.

Roger considered this new information. "Did Alex tell you what he thought we should do?"

"You mean what he thought my friend should do?"

Roger nodded.

"No. I got the impression he felt the best thing would be to return the diamonds through the insurance company. He never explained how. That was probably what he wanted to tell me tonight, but he never got the chance." She looked down sadly. "It's all my fault he's dead."

"You don't know that, Emily. It's likely he was robbed. Isn't that what Detective Hayes thinks? His store was on Main Street. Those things happen."

"I can't imagine anyone hurting Alex. He was liked by everyone, and if someone wanted money, I'm sure he'd give it to them. They wouldn't have to kill him for it. They wouldn't have to torture him like that."

"There are a lot of crazy people in the world, Em."

"It's not safe to go home, Roger. What if the murderer comes there? He's got our name and address. I just don't feel it's safe."

Roger nodded again. "You might be right. How about if we spend the night at the Ramada Inn?"

"What about Lady?"

"It's warm out. She's got her doghouse. She'll be fine."

"Then what? What about tomorrow. We can't live in a motel forever. Isn't it time to go to the police?"

He looked at her somberly, wondering how safe they were. "We'll decide what to do later. Right now, I don't know. Let's think on it for the night."

Emily nodded slowly. "There's one other thing."

"What's that?"

"Alex told me it was an Australian Pink Diamond. They're very rare and very valuable."

The night in the motel was the first time Roger and Emily spent time away from home since January. It felt good to distance themselves from their dilemma, even if only briefly.

Unfamiliar noises woke them several times during the night—evidence that both slept lightly.

When they got up the next morning and left, they were no closer to a solution.

"I hope Lady's OK," Emily said.

Roger turned the car onto their driveway. As they rounded the curve in their driveway, their home came into view. When he didn't see Lady, Roger slowed down.

"What's wrong?" Emily asked.

"Something doesn't feel right." He stopped the car, and backed down the driveway.

"What is it? What are you doing?"

"I'd feel better if I were armed," Roger said, thinking, *whoever murdered JJ and Alex was probably just like Gustafson.*

He drove to Smitty's farm and parked in the driveway, then got out. "Do you want to wait here, Emily, or come inside?"

"I'll wait."

Roger knocked on the door. Smitty opened it a moment later. When he saw Emily in the car, he waved and smiled.

"I'm worried someone may've broken into our house," Roger said. "Can you loan me a rifle?"

"A burglar? You hold on—I'll do you one better." He left the doorway, then came back with two rifles. He handed one to Roger. "I'll follow you."

The two men went to their vehicles. Emily eyed the rifles fearfully wondering if she should've waited at Smitty's house.

When they drove down the Handley's driveway, Lady still didn't come out to greet them.

"Wait here." Roger parked and got out. Smitty was right behind him as they approached the house. Emily rolled down her window halfway so she could hear better.

The back door was closed and unlocked. Roger was sure it was locked when they left. He pushed it open and glanced at Smitty nervously.

"We might be wise to call the cops, Roger," Smitty said.

Roger stepped inside and Smitty walked in right behind him.

The living room was ransacked. Roger saw the same havoc in the kitchen. Furniture was overturned, drawers pulled out and emptied, plants uprooted, and dishes smashed.

"Whoe!" Smitty gasped. Whoever did this was a mean son-of-a-bitch."

Roger nodded. It wasn't a simple burglary. It was obvious someone destroyed the house as if trying to send them a message. The photographs on the mantel had been broken along with everything else. It was vindictive vandalism.

Roger examined the rest of the house and basement. His heart sank when he went out to Emily's office to find it equally destroyed.

Emily saw him through the window and she opened the car door. By then, the men had been in the house for fifteen minutes.

As she got out, she heard a low cry. She looked for the source and found Lady behind the garage, then she screamed.

Roger and Smitty ran to her aid.

"Oh, Emily," Roger said. "It's Lady. That bastard! What did he do?"

Emily moved closer to the dog, which was in great pain. Tears rolled down her cheeks in big drops, falling onto the ground as she reached forward nervously, unsure if she should touch Lady. "She's been stabbed or shot," she said. "There's blood on her coat."

The dog was breathing heavily, its eyes quivering, and its tail still.

Smitty looked at Lady and shook his head. "She's too bad off, Mrs. Handley. She suffering."

Emily looked up in sorrow. "We got to take her to the veterinarian." She looked at Roger, who shook his head.

"No!"

"She's suffering, Em." Roger put his arm around her.

"You two say a quick good-bye," Smitty said. "I'll take care of her. She'll never know a thing. Hurry. I hate to see an animal suffer like this."

Emily and Roger moved closer to Lady. The dog was laboring to breathe. Each breath gurgled in her lungs, and she twitched in pain.

"Oh, Roger, please make it stop!" Emily ran to the house with Roger following. She stopped at the doorway, partly out of shock at hearing Smitty's gun fire, and party from seeing the condition of the house.

Emily gasped. She walked in and looked around in disbelief. Her prize collection of cut glass lay smashed on the floor. Her plants were upturned, and her books lay scattered. Even the paintings on the wall were damaged.

"He was here," Emily whispered.

Smitty came inside. "I'll bury the dog for you. She's already in my truck. Is there any special placed you'd like her?"

Roger shrugged. "I don't know."

"Want me to call the police for you?"

"No!" Roger said too quickly.

Emily glanced at Roger. "We'll call," she said. "We appreciate your help."

"Do you want some help cleaning up? Me and the Mrs. Would be glad to help you. You'd better not touch anything until the police come, though. They won't want it to be disturbed."

"Thanks." Roger walked toward Smitty. "You can have this." He handed Smitty the rifle. I've got my Winchester upstairs."

Smitty accepted the gun and went outside. A moment later, his pick-up drove down the driveway.

Emily and Roger felt vulnerable.

"What can we do, Roger? We have to call the police," Emily said. She tried hard to hold back tears.

"It would be too many coincidences."

"Roger, what can we do? This madman knows something about us. We don't even know who he is. What if there's more than one? We aren't safe anymore."

"Then we can't stay here. Let's get the hell out of here right now." He watched her expression to see if she agreed.

"Where?"

"The cottage."

Her expression brightened. No one knew about their cottage. It was their secret hideaway from work, a haven away from the world.

"Perfect," she said. "Maybe we can think of a way out of this once we get there."

"OK. Let's get out of here fast."

Roger gathered Gustafson's things from the basement while Emily packed clothing in a suitcase. She filled two boxes and a cooler with food. Roger got the cellular phone and boat keys from the garage, along with a few other things they'd need.

Within fifteen minutes, they locked the house and drove down the road toward Maine and their island hideaway.

Eight

They arrived at the marina parking lot in Portland, Maine, shortly after noon. April was early in the boating season, and no one else was around. Usually, the marina owner was working on the boats, but today he wasn't there.

Roger and Emily unloaded their gear from the truck and took it to the dock to reload into their sailboat, *Happy Sails II U.* They were glad no one was there to watch or ask questions.

"It'll take a while to get everything ready," Roger said. "Maybe you should go back to town and get some supplies. It's hard to say how long we'll be out there."

Emily agreed. "I can be back in an hour."

Roger smiled and put his arms around her. They stood on the dock overlooking the ocean. "I love you, Em," he whispered. "I'm sorry about this mess. We'll get out of it somehow. I promise."

Emily squeezed him tightly. "I know." She looked into his eyes for a moment, then left for the store.

One hour later, Roger picked up Emily and the additional supplies from the dock using his dinghy. The sailboat was ready. After stowing the food in the galley, they slipped off the mooring and headed toward Horseshoe Island six miles northeast. It would take an hour to get there using the sailboat's motor, but it was a relaxing, enjoyable ride. They passed smaller islands and ledges along the way.

The warm spring sun was bright on the water, and the tide was low as they passed ledges where seals played and warmed themselves on the rocks. Emily thought sadly of Lady and how she loved the water.

Once they reached the island, their cottage wasn't far. They rounded the point of the island, heading toward Herring Cove, where they'd moor the sailboat.

There were still small patches of snow visible in spots in the woods on the island, and the leaves on the deciduous trees hadn't budded yet. They tied up to the common dock used by the other summer islanders who had cottages there, then unloaded their gear. Roger moved the sailboat to their mooring in the middle of the cove, then motored back to the dock in the dinghy.

It was a thousand-foot walk down a worn path in the woods to their cottage. Roger went to the common shed and retrieved a wheelbarrow for their luggage.

Emily grabbed some bags and started down the path. An almost child-like delight engulfed them as they returned to their summer retreat for the first time in the season. They loved their cottage, and, despite their worry, they soon felt cheerful.

"I wonder what condition we'll find the cottage in?" Roger remembered the mess some squirrels made the previous winter.

The cottage had been closed up since October. It was strictly a summer place, and most people didn't arrive until May or June. Roger and Emily were always the first to come in the spring and the last to leave in the fall.

Everything was as they remembered—the smell of the balsam fir trees and the winding path through the woods. Their cottage was the farthest down the path, making it the most private.

When they arrived, they saw the front windows were still boarded up. They paused to admire the building, then they headed up the small incline to the front porch.

Roger unlocked the door and went inside. It was chilly compared to the outside, and very dark. Emily stayed on the porch until he came back outside.

"We'll need to start a fire," he announced. "it's cold in there. I'll take down the boards so we can get some light."

Emily nodded and set her bags on the porch. They seemed to have gotten heavier during the long walk down the path.

"Why don't you wait out here awhile?" Roger asked. "You'll be warmer."

"Unless you need me, I'll walk near the water," she replied.

"Go on. I'll call you when I'm ready. It'll be warmer in the sun."

Emily went back to the water. The tide was out, and she could see through the crystal water to the rocky bottom near the shore. In the past, she and Lady swam off the nearby large rock. It had a perfect slant for entering and leaving the water. Suddenly, she felt a deep sadness, keenly aware that Lady was truly gone forever. There would be no more throwing sticks into the water for her to fetch.

She worried what would happen to her and Roger as she walked along the shore, skipping shells and rocks into the water. She thought of JJ, Alex, and everything else that happened over the past few months. *Will life ever be like it was?* she wondered.

She sat on a large rock and looked out at the ocean, remembering the words Alex had told her, "*Maybe you should let your friend solve it.*" She wondered if Alex would still be alive if she followed his advice. A tear rolled down her cheek.

She stood and walked along the shore some more.

Emily was sitting on the dock when Roger approached from behind. She didn't turn around, even though she heard him coming.

"The cottage is warm as toast now." He sat down beside her, dangling his feet over the side like Emily.

"It's so peaceful here, Roger. Look out there—nothing but beautiful islands."

Roger gazed out over the seascape. The afternoon sun enhanced the deep blue ocean and cloud-spotted sky. They were in Casco Bay, where hundreds of tiny islands waited for the adventurer, but today, there was no sign of anyone else, not even a lobster boat.

"I'm glad we came," he whispered.

"Me, too." Emily leaned against him, and he put his arm around her. He smelled the freshness of the island and the scent of Emily's hair. To him, that was heaven.

Emily's thoughts were equally tranquil. Here on Horseshoe Island, they always escaped the worries of the world. Somehow, the recent disturbing events they lived through seemed distant, as if they were part of a bad dream one forgot on waking.

If only.

They sat in the sun for a while longer, then they walked back to the cottage. There was still a lot of work to do before dark. With no utilities except a generator, they needed to be ready for nightfall. Lamps needed kerosene, the gas stove in the kitchen needed to be lit, and food needed to be stored or put into coolers.

The tide slowly came back into the cove.

"What about ice?" Emily asked. "We've only got two bags. There was some frozen water on the rocks across the cove. We can use that, can't we?"

"I'll get some." Roger took a hatchet and two plastic pails and then paddled the dinghy across the cove. He reached the frozen stream draping the overhanging ledges and chipped off some chunks of ice.

That worked well. With a large supply of ice, he and Emily felt more secure. They could stay a long time before needing to go back to town.

The combination of the cozy wood stove and the evening darkness made them go to bed early that night. The quiet of the island aided them in getting a much needed sound and restful sleep.

The next morning, barely after sunrise, they woke to the sound of an engine. It was louder than a motorboat, and they thought it might be a low flying airplane. It gradually came closer and got louder.

"What is it?" Emily asked. "It sounds like a helicopter."

Roger got out of bed, pulled on his pants, and looked out the window. He didn't see anything, but the noise was so loud it was almost deafening.

"Get dressed and wait here," he shouted. "I'll see what it is."

He walked out of the room, then came back and took his rifle out from under the bed. Emily was alarmed when Roger set it on the bed.

"If anyone comes…" he began.

"No!" she shouted, shaking her head. The noise was so loud, she couldn't hear him, but she surmised his intention. "I can't!"

He left the rifle and went to investigate. Emily dressed and kept looking out the window.

"What is it?" she wondered. "*Where* is it?" It was so loud it sounded like a helicopter trying to land on the roof.

She went to the front deck and could tell from which direction the noise came. It came from the cove in front of the cottage, from the shore in the cove. She walked closer to investigate, wondering what was keeping Roger.

As she neared the embankment along the shore, she saw an air boat. It had a huge fan on the back to propel it through water and marshlands. She never saw one out there before. The high rocky shoreline of Herring Cove echoed the noise, magnifying it like continuous thunder.

"I hope it's not the murderer." She crept closer, watching intently.

The noise suddenly increased. Emily put her hands over her ears and watched the craft turn and swiftly leave the cove with a man driving it.

A minute later, Roger climbed up over the embankment and came towards her. Emily was relieved.

"Who was that?" she asked.

"Marine patrol. The marina reported our boat missing this morning, and they came to see if we were here." He smiled.

"Maybe we should've told someone we were coming out here," Emily said.

He nodded.

After the morning incident, Roger decided to call his mother, who lived nearby, and tell her they wouldn't be at home for a while, so she wouldn't worry. Emily agreed.

Roger turned on the cellular phone and dialed. "Hi, Mom. How are you?"

Suddenly, his expression changed.

"Really? What did he look like?"

He listened.

"What did you tell him?"

He listened.

"No, that's OK. You did the right thing."

Roger frowned, and Emily felt alarmed.

"Listen, Mom, I have to ask you to do something, and I can't explain why right now."

A pause.

"No, it's OK. Can you go stay with Aunt Jane for a while and not tell anyone where you're going?"

He sighed. "I know it sounds crazy. It's complicated, Mom. I can't explain it right now, but I don't want that man bothering you again."

He listened. Emily waited, biting her nails.

"Please don't say anything about us to him if he asks again. Just say you don't know where we are, OK?"

He frowned again.

"Mom, you don't need to be frightened. Will you please go to Aunt Jane's?"

He looked relieved.

"I'll call you there and I promise to explain it all later. Leave right now, OK?"

"Thanks, Mom. Bye."

"What happened?" Emily asked. "Is she all right?"

"Some man came looking for us. She said he came to her door yesterday and asked if she knew where we were. He claimed it was something about a class reunion, but she described him, and I don't know anyone like that."

Emily bit her lip. "Is she all right?"

"Yes. She'll go to Aunt Jane's in Belfast. She said she'd stay for two weeks. She's been wanting to go for a while, but she sounded a little concerned. I don't know how I'll explain this to her, but I'll figure out something." He sighed.

"Do you think he knows about this place? Did she tell him we might be here?"

"No. She thinks I called from New Hampshire. As far as she knows, we haven't even opened the cottage for the season yet. She said she told him we were visiting friends, but she admitted she didn't like him. He spooked her a little."

"What did he look like?" Emily wondered if that was the man who murdered JJ and Alex.

"She said he was tall, probably six feet, with salt-and-pepper hair. He wore a trench coat with a brown velvet collar and a cowboy hat. She said he drove a real nice car."

"That's it? That could be almost anyone. Maybe he *was* someone trying to get together for a class reunion."

Roger eyed her doubtfully and shook his head.. "Wishful thinking, Em."

She frowned. He was right.

Later that day, Emily brought the phone book out to the porch where Roger sat, deep in thought, watching the ocean. She sat beside him and shared the view.

"What's that?" he asked.

She looked down at the phone book. "Alex suggested the insurance company might be the best way to return the diamonds. We can call anonymously and see what they say."

Roger thought for a moment, then stared at the peaceful ocean scene, where a great blue heron landed gracefully near the shore. "You won't find the number in that book."

She looked at the phone book and realized he was right. "Let's call information."

"What do we ask for, the company that insured a jewelry store that was robbed in New York City last January?"

"I'm just trying to help, Roger! We have to do something. As much as we'd like to, we can't stay here forever."

Roger thought about that. He would've preferred to put the whole thing out of his mind, but she was right. They had to do something, especially if the man was bothering his mother. Roger just didn't want to do anything right then. "Maybe we wouldn't be here if you hadn't decided to *do* something," he said, instantly regretting his words.

Emily stood up and slammed the phone book on the floor. "Fine. You certainly didn't do anything to get us in this mess, did you?" She stomped down the path to the dock.

"Emily, come back! I'm sorry."

She kept walking and went past the dock to the front of the island. She sat on a rock and stared out over the beach. Feeling angry, frustrated, and scared, she cried. She felt guilty about Alex's death, but she couldn't help blaming Roger for getting them into such a mess.

A cold breeze picked up as she sat there. She wondered why Roger hadn't come for her. It had been at least an hour, and the sun was getting low in the sky. She pulled her sweater tighter, thinking her world was crumbling. Perhaps she had betrayed Roger. She wished the whole thing was over.

"There you are." Roger stepped out from the path. "I've been looking all over for you."

She glanced back, then returned her gaze to the beach, staring blankly at the sand and rocks without speaking.

"I'm sorry, Emily. You're right. I got us into this mess. I'm stupid." He sat meekly beside her.

Emily didn't speak.

"I got the number."

"What?" She turned towards him.

"I got the number for the insurance company."

"How?"

"I called information and got a list of Boston insurance companies that specialize in jewelry. It wasn't hard. The third one was it. I spoke to a man named Greeley, the agent in charge of the case. He said he'd meet me and take the jewels, no questions asked, and no one would ever know."

Emily stared. "Just like that? It's that easy?"

"That's what he said. I certainly hope so." He put his arm around her and felt her shivering.

"You're cold. We'd better go back to the cottage."

As they stood up, she hugged him. "I'm sorry I didn't listen to you. It's my fault Alex is dead, and we're hiding out here. If anything happens to your mother, I'll never forgive myself."

"No, Emily. You didn't do anything wrong."

She shook her head.

"Look at me."

She looked into his eyes.

"Mom will be fine. I called her a few minutes ago and she's safe at Aunt Jane's. I don't want you to feel responsible for something I did. I was stupid, and you were just trying to help me, like you've always done. I'm the one who was wrong. Forgive me, please, and don't blame yourself."

They hugged tightly.

"I'll always love you, Roger," Emily whispered, "no matter what happens."

He smiled. "I'll always love you, too."

The next day, Roger and Emily made plans to meet Mr. Greeley in Boston.

"It's off season and warm out," Roger said. "Let's sail down and make an adventure of it. It'll be fun, just the two of us. What do you say?"

She smiled. They loved sailing, and it was very warm for April. "I like it." She touched his hand. "Lets sail to Boston."

"Great. I'll get *Happy Sails* ready. You can pack here, and we'll get started."

"What about Mr. Greeley? When will he expect us?"

"I told him I'd call when we got there to set up a meeting. He's expecting us sometime this week."

Emily nodded. "Sounds good. Do you feel confident you can trust him?"

"I don't have much choice, Em. If it turns out badly, I'll just tell the authorities the truth and hope for the best. At least we're returning the stolen diamonds. That's worth something."

Emily accepted that for the moment. "He actually said he'd meet you alone, take the diamonds, and never reveal who you are?"

Roger nodded. "That's right. I don't want you involved. It's the best option we've got. How else will we get the murderer off our backs? Once the diamonds are returned, there's no reason to pursue us."

"I hope it works."

He smiled. "It will, Em." He walked toward the dock to retrieve the sailboat from its mooring. He secured it to the dock for the night so they could get an early start.

The next morning, they set sail for Boston just after sunrise. Roger motored out of the cover after Emily released the lines. She stood on the bow, hanging onto the stays as the wind blew through her long blond hair.

Once out of Herring Cove, Roger hoisted the mainsail and jib. Emily climbed to the cockpit to snuggle beside him as they sailed toward their destination.

Nine

With favorable winds, Roger and Emily were sailing past the last of the Casco Bay islands by midday. Roger looked at the charts and pointed to a small island. "Let's stop here for lunch," he suggested.

Emily looked at the chart, too. "Sand Dollar Island?"

Roger nodded.

"I wonder if it's called that because of it's circular shape?" Emily asked.

"It could be named for the sand dollars on the beach. Remember when he found some when Tony and Janet were young?"

Emily nodded. "Let's stop."

They dropped anchor and took their dinghy ashore for a brief walk on land.

The island, no more than two acres in size, had a sandy beach on one side and rocky terrain on the other. They climbed up the knoll in the center of the island and sat down for a lunch of sandwiches and fruit.

"We're making real good time," Roger said.

Emily nodded and ate hungrily. The fresh air always enhanced her appetite. "Where are we going to stop for the night?"

"We can probably make it to the Shoals if the winds stay like this."

"That's about halfway, isn't it?"

"Just about. I'll show you the charts when we get back to the boat."

Soon, they were under sail again. The warm spring sun shone on their faces and kept them from getting chilled by the sea breezes until late that afternoon.

By five o'clock, the sun was low in the sky, and the wind died. Roger started the engine so they could motor the final two miles to the Isles of Shoals off the coast of Portsmouth, New Hampshire. They arrived just before six o'clock.

Besides a few fishing boats, they hadn't seen any other boats on the water. It was early in the boating season. Roger pulled the sails down and tied up to a mooring.

Emily prepared dinner while Roger secured the sailboat and studied the charts for tomorrow's sail. "We'll cut through the canal in Ipswich Bay to

BARNES & NOBLE# 1929
MANCHESTER, NH 03103 (603) 627-5766

REG#03   BOOKSELLER#028
RECEIPT#   35273 11/01/97   9:56 PM

S 1879418835   OUT OF SEASON
LIST PRICE: 15.00   1 @ 13.50   13.50

SUBTOTAL	13.50
NO SALES TAX	0.00
TOTAL	13.50
CASH PAYMENT	15.00
CHANGE	1.50

BOOKSELLERS SINCE 1873

Gloucester, making Gloucester by noon, and Boston before dark."

"Are we pushing too hard?" Emily thought it sounded like a tight schedule.

"I don't think so, but we can always stop for another night. I'll call Greeley when we reach Boston. There's no need to rush."

Emily nodded.

They relaxed in the protected cove at the Shoals. There were no other boats nearby, so they were able to tie to a mooring instead of dropping their anchor, which helped them feel more secure for the night.

Sitting in the cockpit, they ate dinner and watched the sun set in a bright pink and orange sky, then went to bed early.

They were ready to depart at dawn, drinking their first cup of coffee as they slipped off the mooring. The huge rising sun was almost as gorgeous as the previous sunset, and a light wind gently filled their sails. Soon, the winds increased and *Happy Sails* moved along at eight knots.

Emily pointed ahead of them. "Look!"

"What is it?" Roger asked.

"Whales!"

Roger loosened the sail for a minute so they could watch the magnificent creatures swim past.

"They're beautiful," Emily said, and she climbed to the bow for a better view. She and Roger marveled at the whales' grace until they swam away.

Roger checked his compass, tightened the sail, and continued on their journey.

A little past ten, they entered the canal leading toward Gloucester, enabling them to avoid rounding the dangerous point of Cape Ann, and saving them many hours of time. They passed the Fisherman Memorial just before noon, and were soon motoring into Gloucester Harbor.

They tied up at a vacant dock for lunch and reexamined their charts. Roger refueled the boat and bought ice for the cooler while Emily prepared supplies for the next phase of their cruise. After eating lunch topside, they continued towards their destination.

As Roger predicted, they arrived in Boston Harbor by late afternoon. That was the first time they'd sailed to Boston, and they watched the sights intently as they slowly motored into the harbor.

"Let's eat out tonight," Roger suggested after they tied to a slip.

"That sounds nice. Where?"

"How about Jimmy's Harborside, or Anthony's Pier Four?"

"Which is closer?" Emily asked, remembering they'd have to walk.

"Jimmy's, I think."

"Sounds great. I'll need to get dressed up."

Roger smiled. "I hope you packed me some nice clothes, too."

Anthony's Pier Four turned out to be closer, and after a gourmet meal, they slowly walked back to their boat.

Emily held Roger's hand and leaned against him. "That was a great dinner. I enjoyed the prime rib. How about you?"

He pulled her close. "The food was great. I'm really full. All that salt air made me hungry. You know, we need to do this more often."

She grinned at him. "I hope you mean taking cruises on the boat."

"Yeah," he laughed. "Without all this other stuff. I've enjoyed this. There are lots of places we can go, especially with business being slow. Why don't we take some time off and enjoy ourselves? We can catch up on work later."

Emily considered the idea as she walked along the shoreline with Roger. The dock leading to *Happy Sails II U* was long, and they weren't in any hurry for the night to end. Both were concerned over what the next day would bring, and hoped it simply meant the end of their ordeal.

"You're right," she said, finally. "We're free to do a lot things right now, with Tony and Janet grown. We might as well do what we want while we're still young enough to enjoy it. Let's plan some trips. We can take weeks to go if you like. It sounds exciting."

The next morning, Roger rose and nervously paced the boat and dock, waiting for Emily to wake up. Finally, she popped her head out of the galley to see what he was doing.

There was a light fog over the harbor, making the landscape eerie. Emily inhaled moist sea air as she looked around.

"How about some coffee?" she asked.

Roger glanced at her.

"Is everything all right?" she asked.

He nodded. "I'm just anxious to get this over with."

"Come down and have some coffee. You'll feel better."

"Maybe you're right." He got back in the boat and went below to the galley.

Emily brewed coffee on the alcohol stove, and Roger removed the phone number he'd scribbled on a piece of the telephone book cover back at the cottage. He nervously turned it over in his hands.

"When will you call him?" Emily asked.

Roger sighed. "I want to wait until ten. What do you think?"

"At least nine. Most people are at work by then."

"All right. I'll call at nine."

The next three hours passed with painful slowness. Emily was sympathetic for Roger and wished she could comfort him, but she didn't know what to say. She kept telling him everything would work out fine, but Roger merely nodded and kept looking nervous.

Finally, at nine o'clock, Roger set the cellular phone on the table and dialed the number.

"Mr. Greeley? I called a few days ago about the stolen diamonds."

Roger frowned. "No, you don't need to know where I am. Do you still want to meet me, so I can turn the diamonds over to you?"

Emily watched and tried to guess what Greeley was saying.

"I'm in Boston, Mr. Greeley, and can meet you this morning if you like."

Emily glanced at the phone and saw the number Roger dialed displayed in the LCD. She glanced back when Roger's face began to flush.

"Look, Greeley, if you want those diamonds back, you'll meet me where I say, not where you say, understand?"

Emily began to bite her nails. She didn't like the tone of the conversation.

"Ok. How about Fisherman's Wharf in twenty minutes?"

Roger nodded, as if Greeley could see him even though he obviously couldn't.

Emily relaxed a little.

"How will I know you?" Roger asked.

"OK. Gray coat and brown hat. NO, I'll find you. Don't worry, I'm as anxious to get rid of these things as you are to take possession of them."

Roger listened.

"Thanks. I'll be there. Twenty minutes." Roger hung up.

"What did he say? You sounded angry. Is everything all right?"

Roger was thinking hard. "Yeah, everything's fine." He slipped the paper back into his pocket. "Do you have the diamonds?"

Emily went into the V berth and retrieved the pouch for Roger. "I polished them for you last night."

"What?"

"You know, so there are no fingerprints on them." She smiled.

Roger nodded. "Good thinking, Em."

"Be careful, Roger."

"I will. I just hope Greeley…" He glanced at Emily. "I'll be glad when this is over."

"Are you sure everything is OK?" Emily was getting concerned.

"Yeah. He tried to get me to meet him someplace, and I didn't like it. He finally agreed to go where I asked, so I should be OK. He's an insurance agent—he must be trustworthy." Roger looked at Emily and saw that she hoped Greeley could be trusted, too, and wondered, briefly, if they weren't both so desperate that they were simply convincing themselves—wishfully hoping, when logic indicated otherwise. He pushed the doubts out of his mind.

Roger checked his watch. "I have to run. He'll be there in fifteen minutes. You wait here. I'll be back in an hour at the most—hopefully sooner."

Roger kissed her quickly. "Don't worry. It's almost over."

He climbed out of the galley and walked down the pier toward Fisherman's Wharf.

Emily stood in the galley to watch him walk away. Once Roger was around a corner and out of view, she went below to clean up. She put the phone back in its spot. Something was bothering her, something felt ominous, but she couldn't quite figure out what it was.

She went into the V berth and got Gustafson's wallet, then sat near the galley table to empty it. The money and his driver's license were still there. Emily studied the photograph and cringed at the sinister face.

She removed the credit cards and examined them, too, temporarily forgetting her concern about Roger's meeting. She remembered there was a key and picked at the wallet until it came out. When it did, she glimpsed a piece of yellow paper she hadn't noticed before. It was stuck behind the cardholder. She pried it out.

It was a small Post-It with a phone number. As she read the number, she felt a surge of adrenaline, but she couldn't understand why. Suddenly, she grabbed the cellular phone and pressed *Redial*.

She gasped when the number Roger had just called appeared on the display. It was the same as the number on the yellow slip of paper from Gustafson's wallet.

"Oh, no! Roger!"

Almost fifteen minutes had passed since Roger left the boat. Emily raced around the corner where she last saw Roger, unsure where Fisherman's Wharf was. She ran down a narrow alley, and a large wharf appeared around the next corner. Roger was in the distance, about two city blocks away. We was walking down a long pier towards a man in a gray coat.

Emily ran down the alley, across the dock, and onto the pier. Roger couldn't see her coming up behind him.

She didn't want Greeley to notice her since she knew he was probably the man who murdered JJ and Alex, and, in his long coat, he was probably the man who visited Roger's mother, too. She wondered how much he knew about Roger and herself.

She wore boating attire—a sweatsuit and comfortable shoes, so she pretended to be jogging. She would reach Roger before he reached Greeley—if she picked up her pace.

Greeley saw Roger coming and walked toward him, wondering who he was and what he really wanted. No one was stupid enough to give away a fortune in Australian pink diamonds. Greeley intended to get the diamonds and make sure no one knew about it. He had no intentions of going back to the office. His supervisor called him in the previous afternoon, but Greeley went out the back door and left. He was on the verge of being fired and didn't want to give his boss the satisfaction.

Roger's call was a shock. Gustafson double-crossed him after the heist, which Greeley planned flawlessly—except for the guards. They weren't supposed to be killed—*damn you, Gustafson!* Greeley rationalized it wasn't his fault.

Adding to his despair was the knowledge that this wife filed for divorce the previous week and told him to leave her life forever. She said she didn't want to be associated with a loser anymore. *I'll show you who's a loser!* he vowed.

He'd been passed over for promotion several times, and he finally decided the only way to get ahead was to take things into his own hands. All he needed to control his destiny was those diamonds and *no witnesses.*

Emily panted as she jogged. Perspiration ran down her forehead and she wiped it away with her sleeve. She hoped she didn't show any fear on her face. Greeley was moving toward Roger, which meant he was heading toward her, too.

She watched as Greeley reached into his large gray overcoat with his right hand.

Roger saw the motion, too, and slowed his walk. He remembered how Gustafson had approached him that same way in the woods. And Greeley's brown cowboy hat? Where had he heard that? Cowboy hat? When Greeley's hand started to come out of his pocket, Roger saw the same crazed look in his eyes, and he stopped dead in his tracks.

Suddenly, Emily ran past Roger. Greeley hesitated to let her go by—no witnesses.

Roger saw Emily and became even more confused. *Why is she here?* he wondered. *What's she up to?* He reached for her, but she was past, heading right for Greeley.

As she approached Greeley, their eyes met, then he ignored her and turned his attention back to Roger. Emily leaped left and knocked Greeley as hard as she could, almost falling over herself.

He fell into the water below the pier.

As he fell, his hand came out with a gun in it, cocked and ready to fire. He tipped over the edge of the dock with a look of horror on his face, then the gun went off. The bullet smacked into the wood under the wharf.

"Emily, what are you doing here?" Roger ran to her. They looked over the wharf, but Greeley was gone. Probably drowned, they hoped.

"Greeley, if that's who he was, knew Gustafson," Emily explained, hanging on to Roger and trying to catch her breath.

"How do you know?"

"I found the same phone number you called on the cellular phone in Gustafson's wallet after you left. He must've known Greeley. Roger, that means Greeley's the murderer! Greeley killed JJ and Alex!"

"Let's get out of here!" Roger looked around, but the isolated wharf was empty, and no one on the shore seemed to have noticed the incident.

They ran back to the boat as fast as they could.

"You go below," Roger said.

Emily handed him a light coat and hat for a disguise, which he put on quickly.

They motored from the slip and into the harbor. Soon, they rounded a small island where they dropped anchor to consider their next move. Thick fog rolled in, and the dock, along with Boston Harbor, disappeared from view.

Ten

They waited for the fog to dissipate, instead it grew denser. They wouldn't be able to travel for a while, but at least no one could find them, either.

After securing the anchor, Roger sat in the cockpit. Emily was beside him.

"I don't believe it," he lamented. "We came all this way for nothing."

"We tried. How could we have known Greeley was in on it?"

Roger grimaced. "I should've suspected something." He made a fist and wished he had something to hit.

After a moment, he went to the bow and stared at the thick fog. He grasped a stay line and tried to think of an answer, but it was as elusive as the fog—constantly moving without lifting.

Shaken by the turn of events, Roger was determined to find a way out.

Emily worried about Roger's state of mind and sensed his desperation. He'd been so certain his ordeal was finally over. What options were left?

"We'll think of something, Roger," she said. "You tried to do the right thing. That's what counts." She walked up beside him.

He shrugged. "I don't know. Maybe you were right all along. Maybe I should go to the police and confess. I can't keep putting you in danger."

Emily felt alarmed. She was afraid for Roger. He was innocent, but who would believe him now? "There has to be a way. All we have to do is get the diamonds back to their rightful owner. Once they've got them back, why would anyone look for us?"

Roger considered that. "I don't know. How the heck can we return them? That insurance agent tried to kill me! Who can we trust?"

She put her arms around him and stared out at the fog. The sea was calm, and the boat rocked gently when other boats passed somewhere out in the harbor. The motion was comforting.

The next morning, they got up at dawn. Neither slept much that night. Without bothering to make coffee, they set sail for Maine and Horseshoe Island. The fog lifted, and the morning sun was bright.

With the wind picking up, there were heavy waves, and Emily watched the ocean with concern.

Roger was a more hearty sailor than she, but she didn't want to add to his tension. She turned on the NOAH weather radio station to monitor the forecast. When it turned out to be favorable, but a bit rough, she relaxed.

By midday they were back to Gloucester and heading through the canal toward New Hampshire. Once past the canal, Roger hoisted the sails, the wind picked up steadily, and Emily went to the bow and held onto a lifeline as she watched the ocean. That was less intimidating than watching the sails tip to the side, and she felt more secure. As she sat there, she got an idea.

Climbing back to the cockpit, she said, "We should return the diamonds to their rightful owner, Roger."

"You mean sail to New York City?"

"We don't have to."

He looked at her.

"I'm pretty sure that jewelry chain has a store in Portsmouth. They had one in Boston, too."

"You mean we could've taken them back while we were in Boston?"

She nodded. "If we'd thought of it."

Roger thought for a moment. "It wouldn't have been wise to hang around with Greeley there."

"Let's stop in Portsmouth," Emily said. "We need supplies, anyway. If there is a store there, we can give the diamonds back. I'm willing to risk it. We've come this far. What do you say?"

Roger paused, squinting his eyes as he looked over the water. He looked at Emily. "Are you sure you want to try it?"

She nodded, smiling. "I'm sure."

He nodded and pressed his lips together firmly. "OK. Let's do it. What have we got to lose?"

Emily went below and tore the page of jewelry stores out of the phone book. She carried it to Roger and showed him there was a branch office in Portsmouth.

"I know the street," Roger said. "We can walk there from Harborplace."

Emily smiled. She climbed back to the bow and resumed her trip, satisfied they had a possible solution.

The winds were favorable and Roger and Emily arrived in Portsmouth by midafternoon, motoring into the mouth of the river. They still had a good four hours of sunlight left. If their errands took too long, they could spend the night at Harborplace, an exclusive marina in the center of Portsmouth that gave easy access to the city. With it being so early in the boating season, there were sure to be plenty of available slips.

Roger secured the boat to the dock and put the pouch of diamonds in his pocket, then walked down the dock toward the street.

"Wait, Roger!" Emily called. "I'm coming with you."

Roger turned. "You should wait here, Em. There's no reason for you to come—we don't know what might happen."

"I'm coming," she said emphatically.

He shrugged.

They walked down the street without speaking. Roger held Emily's hand. Soon, they stood in front of an exclusive jewelry store. The window held some beautiful pieces.

Emily and Roger felt conspicuous standing there in their boating clothes. She smiled at him, understanding his feeling, then they walked inside.

"I'd like to speak to the manager." As Roger spoke, Emily stepped back.

"Do you have an appointment?" the sales woman asked.

"No. But it's very important."

She looked at him, then picked up a telephone at the counter. After speaking softly, she hung up. "He'll see you in a few minutes."

Roger and Emily waited anxiously. Emily looked at the beautiful necklaces and rings behind the glass. A black velvet sign with golden lettering read, *Debeer Diamonds – A diamond is forever.*

Finally, an older man appeared through a back door. He looked at the couple and whispered to his assistant, then walked forward. "What can I do for you folks today?" He asked pleasantly.

Roger was surprised by the man's appearance. He'd always imagined a jeweler as a small, older man with gray hair and thick glasses. The man before him was tanned, average height, and a bit overweight, but he looked athletic and spoke with confidence. His thinning hair was curly and unkempt.

"Is there someplace we can talk privately? It'll only take a few minutes." He looked sincerely into the older man's eyes.

"Sure. Let's go into my office." The man motioned them behind the counter and led them to the back of the shop where his office was.

Roger and Emily felt uncomfortable. It would be a difficult place to escape from if they needed to make a hasty get-away. Emily wondered if she shouldn't have waited in the boat. Roger wished she had.

Once in the office, Roger saw jeweler's equipment on the work area. He pulled out the pouch and wondered what he'd say—how he'd explain the diamonds to this man.

The man sensed his hesitation. "Let me introduce myself." He held out his hand. "I'm James DeMonterio."

Roger shook his hand firmly. "Hi, Mr. DeMonterio. I'm John, and this is...my sister, Lisa."

Emily nodded and smiled weakly.

"What's the nature of your business?" Mr. DeMonterio asked.

Roger hesitated, so Emily stepped forward. "We found some uncut diamonds, and we're certain they came from a robbery of one of your stores." She took the pouch and poured them out on the workbench.

"Is that so?" He looked at the diamonds. "Which store?' He raised his thick, bushy eyebrows.

"The one in New York City, last January," Roger replied.

Emily stepped back behind Roger. Both were nervous, watching the man's reaction.

"You found them? Where?"

Roger glanced at Emily in alarm. They hadn't planned their story. "Along the road near our home."

"That doesn't tell me much, does it?" The jeweler seemed impatient. He picked up one of the stones and held it up to the light, turning it in his fingers.

"We think they're Australian pink diamonds," Emily said, timidly.

He laughed. "Australian pinks?"

Roger glanced at Emily, puzzled by the jewelers comment and less-friendly demeanor. "Are the diamonds flawed?" he asked.

Mr. DeMonterio kept examining the diamonds. "Australian pink diamonds are extremely rare. Carat for carat, they're worth more than twenty times the value of other diamonds." He held up one. "One this size is worth over two million dollars."

Roger and Emily exchanged glances. There were twelve diamonds in the pouch, all as large or larger than the one he held up. If what he said was true, they could be worth over twenty-four million dollars!

DeMonterio placed the diamond under a scope, then sighed. "What do you two want? Do you think I'll pay you for these?"

Roger was taken aback and wondered if they'd made a mistake. Emily was confused, too.

"We don't want money, Mr. DeMonterio," Roger said.

Emily nodded.

"Then what exactly **do** you want?" He looked into Roger's eyes.

"We want to give them back to their rightful owner. We don't want them. That's all."

Mr. DeMonterio's lips pressed together as he studied them. "I see." There was disgust in his voice.

"We tried going to the insurance company," Roger explained, "but that didn't work. We wanted to go to the police, but we couldn't without implicating ourselves—and we *aren't* implicated. We were just in the wrong place at the wrong time. That's the truth."

"Of course. You just want to return them now, is that is?"

They nodded, mystified. Why wasn't this man happy to get the stolen merchandise back?

Mr. DeMonterio placed one of the diamonds on his workbench, picked up a small hammer, and struck hard. The diamond shattered into tiny pieces.

Roger's jaw fell open. Emily gaped. They looked at Mr. DeMonterio, then each other.

"I don't know who played a trick on you two," Mr. DeMonterio said, "but someone's having a good laugh at your expense."

"They're fakes!" Emily said.

"All of them?" Roger asked.

"Every single one. Want me to prove it?" He raised the hammer again.

"No, that's OK." Emily put the stones in the pouch and tucked the pouch into her jacket pocket, still attempting to keep the evidence in a safe place, knowing how illogical that seemed to be.

"I don't understand." Roger was stunned. "We've been burglarized, stalked, and attacked for those diamonds! Why? They're fakes! All along, they've been fakes."

Mr. DeMonterio motioned for them to sit down. They did, reluctantly. He now seemed genuinely concerned about them.

"Let me tell you something no one knows yet," he began. "The real diamonds from that robbery were recovered yesterday from a man who sells stolen gems in Boston."

"All of them?" Emily asked, thinking of Greeley.

"Yes. These are duplicates. They're good, but they're fakes. The originals are in a vault in New York City."

They sat in silence for a moment. Roger and Emily were in shock. Mr. DeMonterio studied them carefully.

"Have you got a few minutes?" he asked.

They nodded slowly.

He picked up the telephone receiver, pressed a button, and hung up. A tone sounded, then the phone automatically dialed and rang. A woman answered on the speaker phone.

"Good afternoon, this is Kay."

"Kay, Monty here."

"Monty! How are you today?"

"Fine." He nodded. "Put me through to the big guy, OK?"

"Sure. Hold on."

Roger and Emily sat quietly and listened. A man's voice sounded on the speaker a moment later.

"Monty! What's up?"

"Stewart, I've got a question for you." DeMonterio had a gleam in his eye as if he knew a secret.

"Shoot."

"Those diamonds that were recovered yesterday weren't Australian pinks, by any chance, were they?"

There was brief silence as Mr. DeMonterio grinned at Roger and Emily.

"How'd you know that?" the man asked.

"Let's just say I heard a rumor. So, it's true?"

"Yes, but no one knew. It was strictly an inside job. We know whoever pulled it off was privy to confidential information."

"Greeley!" Roger blurted.

"Is someone with you, Monty?"

Mr. DeMonterio motioned Roger to keep silent. "I said that, Stewart."

"How did you know about Greeley?"

Mr. DeMonterio paused.

"Another rumor?" Stewart sounded skeptical.

"An inside job? Have they made any arrests?" Mr. DeMonterio asked.

"The fence was arrested with the diamonds last night. It turns out two others are wanted. We're pretty sure Greeley, the insurance agent, planned it, because he had knowledge of the shipment. It was insured for twenty-eight million. We're also after a thug named Brian Gustafson. He actually pulled the heist and killed the two guards. We got him on the surveillance video. They think there's one more person involved, but we don't know who yet."

Emily glanced at Roger and knew he was thinking the same thing she was—*the other person was JJ.*

"Thanks for the info, Stewart. When are you coming up this way? I'll take you out on my boat."

"Sounds good. Can't resist an offer like that. Maybe next month. I want to know where you heard that rumor."

"Take care, Stewart."

"Bye."

The line went dead. Mr. DeMonterio pushed a button and turned off the speaker. "I hope that answers some of your questions."

Roger looked at Emily. "That means we're safe now, Em. It's over. We can go home."

"Em?" The jeweler grinned. "What's up with you two? You don't strike me as the criminal type. What's this about Greeley—the insurance agent?"

"It's a long story. Thank you, Mr. DeMonterio. You've helped us more than you know," Roger said, standing up. Emily followed.

She smiled gratefully at the jeweler. "Thanks." She shook his hand.

He shrugged. "Good luck, whatever it is."

They hurried out of the store.

Walking back to Harborplace in the warm afternoon sunlight, Roger and Emily felt relieved. Emily glanced at Roger and they both laughed.

"It's over!" he said. "I can't believe it."

As they headed for the dock, they admired the quaint old historic buildings of Portsmouth. They'd overlooked them when they arrived earlier. Now the world seemed brighter and they felt like skipping back to the dock.

"Let's get some lobster for dinner," Roger suggested. "We could go out to the Shoals and spend the night there, then head back to the island tomorrow morning."

"I like it."

They got supplies and fuel, then motored back down the river toward the open ocean. It was a clear afternoon, and they reached the Isles of Shoals, a six-mile sail, just as the sun set. They watched another pink and orange array as they happily sipped champagne.

Eleven

Roger lit the lantern and began boiling water on the alcohol stove for the lobsters. Emily prepared the vegetables and salad and set the small table in the galley as elegantly as she could. The evening was cool, so she handed Roger a sweater, which he slipped on gratefully. Soon, they were ready to eat in the galley.

Roger held up his glass of wine for a toast. "To a normal, uneventful life!"

Emily smiled back, her blue eyes sparkling in the dim light. "To a wonderful life."

After touching glasses, Roger leaned over and kissed her. She closed her eyes and enjoyed the feeling of closeness.

Suddenly, Emily cocked her head at a faint sound. "What's that?"

Roger listened. "Sounds like a motorboat. It's probably a fisherman going home after dark."

The boat came closer as they ate. "I'm going to take a look," Roger said, climbing out of the galley into the cockpit. There was a motorboat approaching, so Roger watched and waited, not expecting much.

Emily stayed near the opening to the galley, watching but anxious to get back to their meal. The moon was rising like a huge silver nickel, shimmering over the gently moving ocean. She went below.

As the motorboat neared, Roger had a feeling something wasn't right. Then he recognized the operator of the boat—it was Greeley!

"God, what can he want?" Roger asked. "Em, stay below. It's Greeley. Let me find out what he wants."

"Greeley? Are you kidding?" She peered out the small galley window to see what was happening.

Greeley pulled up beside the sailboat and tied a line loosely to one of the stays. Roger noticed he wasn't wearing his cowboy hat and surmised he'd lost it at the dock when he fell into the water. He watched as Greeley stepped on board.

Greeley pulled out a revolver.

"Wait a minute, Greeley. What do you want with us? We don't have the diamonds."

"You know exactly what I want. Give me those diamonds, or you're dead."

"Greeley, you're making a big mistake! They're…"

"No! You're making the mistake."

Emily crept into the V berth and retrieved the pouch from her jacket pocket, then she climbed out the forward hatch and stood on the bow. Greeley saw her, but his gun remained on Roger, who was six feet away. Both boats rocked in the water, gently banging together.

"I've got them!" Emily said.

"Emily, what are you doing?" Roger shouted.

"Shut up!" Greeley eyed Emily. "Give them to me right now."

"Drop your gun or I'll let these go into the ocean." She leaned over the bow with her right arm wrapped around a stay line. Her left hand stretched out over the water.

Greeley peered at her angrily. "Give me the diamonds, or you'll be dead like your friend in the shop."

Emily felt sick. "You mean Alex?"

"Is that his name? He didn't want to tell me where the diamonds were. I thought he had them until I saw your name on his pad. He seemed nervous about that. It was convenient of you to leave your card." He laughed and pulled Emily's blue business card out of his pocket, then tossed it into the water.

Emily watched it float by. The ocean's blue surface was luminescent in the bright moonlight. She looked at him and their eyes met. "You killed JJ, too, didn't you?" She wanted to stall, giving Roger time to think of something.

Greeley laughed. "The only one I haven't killed is Gustafson, that son-of-a-bitch! Where is he?" He looked back at Roger.

Roger watched the scene unfold in disbelief. "He's dead."

Greeley eyed him suspiciously. "You aren't trying to tell me that a hick like you killed a man like Gustafson? I doubt it. He's trying to double-cross me. He took the diamonds, but I'll get him for that. He'll pay." His face contorted in anger.

Roger glanced at Emily who was still leaning over the bow. Greeley wouldn't let them live after confessing to two murders. There was no doubt about his intentions to kill both of them. Roger's heart pounded, and his palms were damp. He had to save Emily, somehow.

Greeley looked at Emily. "Hand them over."

"You were involved in the robbery in New York, weren't you, where those two guards were killed?"

Greeley chuckled. "I wasn't involved. I masterminded the whole thing. Gustafson screwed it up. No one would've been hurt if he did what I told him." He pressed his lips together.

Emily glanced Roger a panicked, **come on, think of something** look.

"That doesn't matter anymore." Greeley said. "I waited long enough for my chance, and I took it.

You two sure won't keep it from me. I don't know what you're up to, but you won't get away with it. You never should've messed with me."

He steadied his gun at Roger while looking intently at Emily. There was fear on her face as he pulled back the hammer with his thumb and cocked the gun.

Emily turned the pouch slightly, and one diamond fell into the water, sparkling as it sank out of sight.

Greeley was shocked, then he glared at her. "He's dead if you don't give them to me right now!" he bellowed.

Emily gulped, holding the pouch as far out over the water as she could reach, and still steady herself with the stay.

Roger wiped his hands on his pants.

"Ok," she said. "I'll give them to you." She looked at both men, then brought the pouch slowly toward herself with her left hand. She clumsily tied the pouch securely as she swayed over the water, her right arm still looped around the stay line.

She looked intently at Greeley, then tossed him the bag. "Here." She threw it behind him so he'd have to reach to catch it.

Greeley was caught off guard and instinctively grabbed for the pouch. He wasn't able to keep his gun on Roger and catch simultaneously. In panic, he only thought about the diamonds.

Roger lunged for him, knocking them both off the side of the sailboat. Greeley fired wildly, clutching the pouch of diamonds, then both men struck his motorboat as they fell into the ocean.

Emily screamed as they hit the dark water. She hurried along the side of the sailboat toward the spot where the men fell in, wondering if Roger was hit by the shot.

"Roger! Where are you?" she shouted.

Roger surfaced. The cold water stunned him briefly when he fell in. He gasped from the biting cold. "Where's Greeley?" He clung to the side of the motorboat and looked around, shaking from the cold.

Emily shrugged. "I don't know. I can't see him. Are you OK?" She looked into the ominous dark water.

Roger hauled himself into the motorboat and looked around. "There he is." He dived in.

"Roger! What are you doing?" Emily cried.

She watched fearfully as Roger surfaced again holding a limp body. Emily climbed into the motorboat to help pull Greeley in.

"Is he dead?" she whispered.

Roger checked for a heartbeat and found none. He rolled Greeley over and saw his neck was broken from the fall. They covered him with a tarp and climbed back aboard their own boat. Roger shivered from the cold water. Emily covered him with a blanket.

"Why'd he come after us?" Emily asked. "The diamonds were returned."

"He didn't know. I'll bet he thought we called his company and told them about him. He must not have gone back to work, or he would've known. Somehow, he followed us here."

Emily looked at the boat and Greeley's body. "Now what? How do we explain this?"

Roger went below to change, and Emily helped him. "We don't explain it, Em."

"What do you mean?"

Later that night, under the light of the full moon, Roger and Emily tied the motorboat securely to the sailboat, then slipped from their mooring and towed the boat beyond the Isles of Shoals to where the water was extremely deep.

Emily watched as Roger turned off their engine. Soon, they drifted under a moonlit sky. They felt the gentle swells of the open ocean. Behind them, silhouetted in blackness, were The Shoals.

Roger jumped onto the motorboat and secured Greeley's body to the seat with some rope. Then he took an ax and started chopping at the bottom of the boat.

Emily glanced around anxiously. They were alone. Within minutes, the motorboat began filling with water. Roger jumped back into the sailboat and untied the motorboat.

The two boats slowly drifted apart, then the motorboat filled with water and silently slipped below the surface. Roger and Emily watched the empty ocean where the boat had just been. Emily leaned close to Roger, who wrapped his arms around her to keep her warm.

"Did we do the right thing?" she whispered.

He swallowed. "He would've done the same to us, Em. Look what he did to Alex and JJ. It's the right thing."

They quietly hoisted the sails and headed back toward The Shoals. Greeley's cowboy hat pried loose from under the motorboat's front bow seat where he'd secured it, and bobbed to the surface, floating in the shadows as they sailed away.

Even though they were anxious to return home, it wasn't safe trying to travel in the dark The ocean sparkled with moonlight as they headed to the safety of the mooring.

"I hope that's the end of it." Emily said, glancing at Roger, who steered the sailboat from the cockpit.

"There isn't any other link with Greeley gone," Roger said. "He was Gustafson's partner in the crime. Who else could link us?"

Emily thought for a moment, then went below. She came out a moment later with Gustafson's wallet and beeper. "What about these things? Let's sink them, too, while we're out in the deep water."

Roger opened the wallet. "No need to waste good money." He stuffed the bills into the back pocket of his jeans. As he did, the key fell out and clanged against the cockpit floor.

Emily groped for it in the shadows. Instead of handing it to Roger, she cocked her arm, ready to throw it away.

"Wait!"

She stopped in surprise and lowered her hand. "What is it, Roger?"

Roger tossed the wallet and beeper overboard. They watched them sink, then Roger said, "Let me see that key."

Emily handed it to him. "What is it?"

"What if..." He thought fast. "What if Gustafson fenced the stolen diamonds before that day in the woods?"

"So?"

"What if he hid the money somewhere? Maybe this key would tell us where it is." Roger looked at her in excitement.

"Wouldn't that implicate us?" she asked. "If we found the money, which I doubt, wouldn't that be hard to explain?"

"I know it's a long shot, but just think. Someone fenced the diamonds, or they couldn't have been recovered. Remember what Mr. DeMonterio said? They were recovered from a man in Boston."

"Gustafson had the diamonds, so he must've sold them while he was still in Boston. That's where Detective Hayes said he rented the car, remember? I'll bet this key goes to a locker somewhere. If we can find it, that'll answer our question."

"You still haven't answered my question, Roger. How would we explain the money?" She didn't want to admit she was excited, too. If DeMonterio was right, the diamonds were worth over twenty-six million dollars. Even a fraction of that was a lot of money.

"What's to admit? We could anonymously donate it to charity, or we could use some of it to put our life back together. There's a mess waiting for us back home, don't forget."

Emily sighed. "It's a bit if. I don't see how we'd ever find the right locker, if it even exists."

"Are you willing to try?" Moonlight twinkled in his eyes.

Emily smiled. "I'm game if you are."

Roger put the key in his pocket.

Twelve

The fair weather ended as they returned to Horseshoe Island. They tied *Happy Sails II U* to the dock and raced down the path to the cottage as huge raindrops started falling. They felt like children and raced each other to the porch where they collapsed, wet and laughing.

"Cold?" he asked.

Emily smiled. "A little."

Roger moved closer to her. "I love you, Em. I've put you through a lot, but I'm glad you stayed with me."

Emily kissed him gently, then stroked his cheek. "I'm nothing without you in my life. Just promise me you won't go hunting out of season again."

They laughed.

"I promise," he said. "I'll never do anything so stupid again, Em. I don't know what I was thinking. I've been racking my mind trying to figure out why I did it."

"In the end, it might've been for the best."

"What do you mean?"

"If Gustafson hadn't met JJ that day, and come to our house looking for him, we would've been in danger, especially if he mistook you for JJ."

Roger nodded. "That's possible. He was a bad guy. I wouldn't want you to meet him. He made Greeley look like a Boy Scout."

He felt her shaking. "You're shivering. Let's go inside and start a fire."

Roger and Emily waited until the next day for the rain to subside. They'd been away from home for over a week, and both were anxious to return to New Hampshire and get things back in order. Roger called his mother at Aunt Jane's house and told her it was safe to return home. The rest of the explanation would wait until later.

They left the marina in Portland, Maine, in midmorning the next day and were soon back in New Hampshire. They thought of Lady as they drove down the driveway and missed her usual greeting.

They began the arduous task of cleaning up their vandalized home. By the end of the day, most of the broken things were discarded, and the house looked normal again.

The next day, Emily worked in her office. She had much catching up to do, and spent most of the day replacing files and straightening papers.

Roger came into her office at five o'clock. "How about if I fix dinner tonight?" He looked around. "You did a lot. The place looks great."

Emily smiled weakly. "Thanks. What did you plan to make?" She gladly accepted his offer.

"It's a surprise, but don't worry, you'll like it."

Roger turned to go.

"Thanks, Roger. I'm really tired and don't know what I'd make for dinner."

"That's OK, Em. No problem." He knew she was discouraged. The damage had been more than they expected. He went inside, and Emily finished the last of her straightening.

She surveyed the office when she finished, satisfied it was workable again. There were several phone messages on her machine, so she decided to write them down.

There were four calls from Emily's clients, beginning with Norman, and two calls from Roger's mother.

She listened intently as his mother asked, "Roger where are you? There's a man looking for you. He's been here twice and says it's important he talk to you soon. Call me when you can. Bye."

Emily cringed when she realized that call came from her mother-in-law before they set sail for Boston, when Greeley visited her.

Another message was from Smitty, asking if they were all right.

The last one was from Norman again. "Emily, I've been by several times. Did you get my Financial Statements ready? I need to talk to you right away. I hope everything's all right. Call me."

The urgency in Norman's voice indicated he was worried he wasn't her number-one priority. She smiled and thought how nice it was to have things back to normal.

She looked at her list and made a mental note to call Norman the first thing in the morning. She'd tell him they were called away to help relatives in Maine.

She sighed. Even though she was behind in her work, she was back to her old routine, and it felt good. Tomorrow, they'd resume their normal life. There would be no more close calls with murderers. She loved Roger and was glad it was finally over.

Roger made spaghetti dinner for Emily, complete with garlic bread and tossed salad. He was delighted everything worked out and vowed never to risk everything he loved again.

As they ate, Emily pointed out the dining room window. Standing in the field in front of their house was **the buck**. His antlers were silhouetted against the evening sky as he nibbled on shoots in the field. It was almost as if he were greeting them on their return home.

"He's still there," Roger said fondly.

"Do you think you really would've shot him? He's so beautiful."

"I wonder." Roger stared out the window thoughtfully.

The next morning, Roger helped Emily get caught up. As she hurried to run a load of laundry, he went out to get the mail. Emily emptied Roger's pockets and found the key. She examined it briefly, then put it into her sweater pocket before starting the washer and walking back to her office.

Roger returned with a large handful of mail and delivered it to Emily's office. She put the key on her desk next to the phone, then thumbed through the mail. As they talked, a car came into their driveway. Roger's eyes widened when he looked up.

"What is it?" Emily asked.

"It's the police!"

"Do you think Smitty told them about the vandalism?" Emily asked.

Roger looked at her. "Oh, no."

Detective Hayes walked into her office a moment later. "How are you folks?"

Emily smiled. "We're fine, Detective. It's nice to see you again."

Roger marveled at how calm she was. His palms were damp, and he imagined all kinds of terrible scenarios, from being arrested for Gustafson's death to being implicated in the robbery.

"I stopped by to let you know how we're doing with the investigation of JJ's death and the abandoned car."

"Oh, yes. What did you find out?" Emily asked.

Roger sat in a nearby chair to listen.

"We feel the man who rented the car was a felon named Brian Gustafson. He was also the man who shot your neighbor." He watched Emily's reaction carefully.

"Really?" She feigned surprise and glanced at Roger. "Go on."

"It seems your neighbor was involved in some risky business—buying stolen jewelry. He got in over his head this last time. We've been watching him for a while, and we guess he must've met with Gustafson, and they disagreed over something. Gustafson was known for his brutality, and he probably killed JJ in anger or for spite. We might never know. Anyway, he fenced the stolen diamonds in Boston, and they were recovered."

"Really?" Emily repeated.

"I just wanted to let you know. There shouldn't be any danger to you, and I'm sure Gustafson's far away by now. The Boston police told us that his accomplice, a man named Greeley, is missing, too. Those two are long gone, probably enjoying their loot on some exotic island. You'll be safe."

"I'm sure they are," Emily said. "We appreciate you coming by to tell us."

"I came by a few times, but you were gone. Took a vacation?"

"Yes. We went to Maine to visit my husband's relatives. I was pretty shook up after Alex's death, and needed to get away."

"Is that so?" He eyed the key Emily left on her desk.

"I know what you two have been up to," Hayes said, loudly.

Roger glanced at Emily, who swallowed hard as Detective Hayes reached for the key. He held it up and grinned. "You can't fool me. I'm a detective."

Silence permeated the room. He eyed Emily and Roger, saw their guilty expressions, and said, "Ha!" as he tossed the key back down on the desk.

"What do you mean, Detective?" Emily asked.

"You don't lie very well," he said.

"I don't understand," she stammered. Roger grabbed the arm of his chair.

"You've been to Logan Airport. Tell the truth—you went south for the warm weather, didn't you? Look, you're both tanned."

"Logan?" Emily's eyes brightened.

"This key's from a locker at Logan Airport, isn't it? I had one just like it last month when I flew out of there."

"Oh? We didn't know," Emily said.

Roger spoke quickly. "It's our son, Tony's key. He left it here at Christmas time. We were wondering where it belonged."

"I'll be." Detective Hayes picked up the key again and studied it carefully. "It's from Logan, all right. I'd bet on it."

He glanced at Roger. "There's a time limit on those lockers. If your son has anything valuable there, you'd better get it soon." He smiled and set the key back down on Emily's desk.

Emily and Roger sighed in relief. There was a twinkle in their eyes as they looked at each other, both wondering if Gustafson hid the money in a locker at Logan Airport.

Detective Hayes nodded as if he understood and was glad to have helped them solve a mystery. "We need more concerned citizens like you, Mrs. Handley. If you ever notice anything unusual in the neighborhood again, call. Maybe, if we got on the case sooner, we might've saved JJ."

"What about Alex?" Emily asked, regretting it the moment the words left her mouth, but unable to stop.

"The store owner?"

"Yes. Do you have any leads to his killer? He was a dear friend."

The detective sighed. "Unfortunately, it's a hard case to solve. Right now, we're calling it robbery gone bad. To tell the truth, we might never know. You haven't remembered anything that might help, have you?

She shook her head. "If I do, I'll call right away. Alex wouldn't have hurt anyone. I still can't believe someone murdered him."

"I just wanted to let you folks know so you don't worry anymore." He turned to go. "Take care."

"Thanks, Detective Hayes." Roger stood and held out his hand, smiling. "Thank you *very* much."

The detective shook it heartily. "You're welcome, sir."

A moment later, he drove out the driveway.

"Whew!" Roger sank into a chair.

"It was a good thing I was cautious about that car," Emily said. "It helped you seem more innocent."

"I know. At the time, I thought it would tip them off to Gustafson being in the well."

"We'll have to do something about that," Emily said.

He agreed. "I'll rent a backhoe and fill it in before anyone finds him. I'll have to wait a bit—it's too wet to go out there with all the spring rain."

"I'll be glad when that's done. No more loose ends."

Roger nodded.

The next day, Emily mentioned the locker key when Roger came into her office.

"I don't know about you, but I'd like to solve the last piece of the puzzle," she said. "Do you want to play detective this weekend?"

"The chance that Gustafson hid the money in that locker seems remote. It could be a total waste of time."

Emily frowned. "I'd still like to try. What if he did?"

Roger smiled. "Ok, Em. We can eat at the Hill Top, so the trip won't be a complete waste. Just don't get your hopes up. It'll probably be a wild goose chase."

Secretly, Roger was as excited as Emily.

On Friday night, Roger and Emily had dinner and saw a movie with friends. Roger laughed and enjoyed the evening, feeling like his old, guilt-free self. Emily caught his eye occasionally, as if reading his mind. She was glad to see him back from the world of deception and despair he fell into.

Later, as they prepared for bed, Roger watched Emily brush her long blonde hair. "You were beautiful tonight."

She smiled. "I had a nice time. Didn't you?"

He nodded. She got up, turned off the light, and slipped into bed beside him. He put his arm around her as she cuddled closer. They were excited about their trip in the morning.

"Do you think we'll find the locker?" Emily smiled at the thought of whispering in the house with the children grown and gone.

"We might."

"Gustafson may've taken a plane from New York. He rented the car in Boston and had to get there somehow," Emily said

"I hope you won't be disappointed," he said.

"What do you mean?" She raised up on one elbow to look into his eyes.

"We might not find anything," he said.

"I know it's a long shot, but it'll be a nice day. We'll have dinner at the Hill Top and see some of the sights. It'll be fun. I'm not really expecting to find anything."

"Good." He kissed her.

They skipped their usual morning jog and ate a small breakfast.

Emily gazed out the window as she chewed her toast. "Should we get another dog?" she asked. "I miss Lady, don't you?"

Roger nodded sadly. "If you'd like a dog, so would I. A puppy?"

She thought about that. "Let's check the animal shelter next week. There might be a nice dog that needs a home."

"Sounds good."

As they locked the door to leave, Roger asked, "Do you have the key?"

She patted her purse. "It's right here."

Boston was over an hour away. Even though it was a weekend, traffic was heavy, especially compared to rural New Hampshire. Roger finally got them to Logan Airport and parked in the main garage.

They walked through the main entrance and looked around.

"Where are the lockers?" Emily whispered.

Roger studied the area. "Let's look over there." He pointed toward a long hallway to the left. They walked down the corridor, searching for lockers.

They passed an airport worker.

"Where are the storage lockers?" Emily asked.

The young man answered in broken English, directing them back to a rest area in the main lobby.

"Thank you." Emily smiled.

They hurried back and found some lockers, but the key number didn't match any of the spaces they found.

"It's not here," Roger said, surprised.

"Shucks. Now what?" Emily said.

"I told you not to get your hopes up."

"I know, and I told you the same thing. Still, I wish we'd found it. Then we'd know for sure." She looked at the lockers on the wall. "This doesn't seem like enough for a large airport."

"Maybe there's more than one location. What if each wing has its own lockers?"

They hurried to find out.

Eventually, they found three other storage areas, but none had the correct locker. Roger asked another attendant if there were any more locker areas. There weren't.

"That's that," Roger said. "We tried."

Emily squeezed his hand. "Don't feel bad, Roger. Gustafson probably never put the money in a locker, anyway. I'm hungry. Let's go to the Hill Top."

"I'm with you." He glanced at his watch and saw it was just past noon. "I hope it's not mobbed."

At the Hill Top Restaurant, they had a short wait, then they were seated in the Tucson Room. Each dining area had a Western name. They placed their order and waited for it to arrive.

"It's for the best," Emily said, breaking the silence.

"What?"

"That we didn't find the money. Remember how we felt when we had those diamonds? We couldn't wait to get rid of them."

"That was different. The diamonds linked us to a robbery and to Gustafson. I wouldn't feel the same way about the money."

Emily realized Roger had been hoping to find the money. She thought that was because he'd been out of work for so long and wanted to contribute to the household income, or perhaps he hoped to compensate for the ordeal they went through. She sighed.

The waitress brought them their T-bone steak dinners, and they enjoyed the meal immensely, forgetting the key and their frustration. They chatted happily about their plans for the summer and upcoming visits with their children.

As they drove back to New Hampshire, they thought about what happened. Neither said anything, not wanting to admit they were puzzled about the key. Emily began to wish she'd tossed it overboard that night and ended the speculation.

A large bus passed them as they went through Manchester. That gave Roger an idea. He saw a road sign and took an exit to follow the bus.

"Why are we getting off here?" Emily asked.

"Just a hunch."

"What?" She looked at him.

He didn't answer, just continued down the road. Soon, Emily saw a sign that read, *Airport.*

She raised her eyebrows. "Are you going to the Manchester airport? Do you think Gustafson went here? It's so far out of the way—why would he do that?"

"Yes, but what if he got this far and realized he had the money in the rented car and didn't want to leave it while he traipsed through the woods to meet JJ?"

"I doubt that. It's a pretty wild guess, Roger."

"Do you remember when the rental company came to get the car in January? They were from Manchester, even though he rented the car in Boston. Maybe he planned to return the car to Manchester all along. Maybe he planned to take a flight out of

Manchester after meeting JJ. He may've stored his loot here instead of at Logan. There's no need to drive all the way back to Boston when he could've taken a plane from here. Since we're here, let's check it out."

Emily shrugged. "OK."

"Wait here." Roger parked in a loading zone and walked quickly into the terminal.

Emily waited several minutes, and began to worry. She looked around often, hoping she wouldn't have to move the car before he got back.

The Manchester Airport was much smaller than Logan in Boston. Roger located the locker section of the airport and began searching for a number that matched the key. He found it.

As Roger inserted the key, a man approached from behind. "Just what do you think you're doing?"

Roger jumped. Slowly he turned around to face the blue-and-white uniformed man. "What's the problem, sir?" he asked.

"Problem? You didn't think you could just walk in here, get your stuff and leave, did you?"

"Huh?" Roger shifted his weight nervously.

"You owe six months rent on that locker! We were just about to open it up and confiscate the contents. Lucky you came today, buddy, or you'd never see your stuff again."

"Six months rent?" Roger smiled and relaxed..

"That's right. Before I let you haul off your belongings, you better cough it up."

"How much?" Roger asked, reaching for his wallet.

"Sixty dollars." The clerk pulled out a pad from his pocket and began writing.

Roger handed him the money and the clerk gave him the receipt.

"Been nice doing business with you," the clerk said, turning away.

"Same here," Roger said, turning around to open the locker.

Emily tapped on the dash board nervously. "Where is he?" Finally, she saw him coming out the terminal doors. He carried a duffel bag.

"I don't believe it," she said.

Roger opened the rear door and tossed the heavy bag onto the seat. He smiled at Emily, who was amazed.

"A piece of cake," he said, closing the back door. He got in the driver's seat and drove away.

"You found the locker? I don't believe this! What's in the bag? Did you look?"

Roger was driving carefully through the traffic. "I haven't looked. I just wanted to get out of there as fast as I could. The bag's really heavy."

Emily reached over the back of the seat and dragged the duffel bag into her lap. It was large and awkward with the two of them sitting in the front seat. She unzipped it.

There were some clothes and books on top which she tossed onto the floor, then she pulled out a small paper bag. She glanced at Roger, who was as curious about the contents as she was. She reached into the bag, smiled, and looked at Roger as she pulled out a large bundle of money.

"These are hundred-dollar bills!" she exclaimed. "There must be a hundred of them in this bundle!"

She dumped out the bag, revealing another nineteen bundles and did some quick calculations.

"How much?" Roger asked excitedly.

"There are two hundred thousand dollars in this one bag, and there are more bags in the duffel!"

"How many more bags?" He glanced at the duffel bag and back to the road.

Emily reached into the duffel bag and counted three rows of twelve bags. "There are thirty-five more bags. If they're all the same, it means we've got eight million dollars!"

She glanced at Roger. "Oh, my God, Roger."

"Be careful no one sees you." He watched cars passing them on the interstate as he drove up the ramp to merge with the traffic.

Emily replaced the money and other items in the duffel bag. "Alex was right. They *were* Australian pink diamonds."

"Mr. DeMonterio said they were worth more than twenty times as much as regular diamonds. That's amazing," Roger said.

"I can't believe you found the money. You were right. Gustafson hid it before reaching Concord."

"Now all we have to do is decide what to do with it." He glanced a Emily. "I've got a few ideas."

She grinned. "Tell me."

"I'll explain when we get home."

Epilogue

The sun was bright and warm. Roger, Emily, and their guests were cooled just enough by the gentle ocean breezes to be comfortable. *Happy Sails II U* rocked gently at anchor in a small protected cove near their island in Casco Bay.

Roger checked the coals on the grill. "They're ready! I can cook the steaks anytime."

Emily smiled and turned away from Helen to answer him. "Be right with you, Dear."

"I like what you've done to the boat," George said.

Roger beamed. He was proud of his sailboat. The new teak wood and sails really improved its appearance.

Emily brought the steaks to Roger in the cockpit.

"I'm going below for a few minutes," George said and left.

"Trixie, you can't have these," Emily said to the excited dog. "You have to wait."

Emily watched George go into the galley where Helen was. She leaned close to Roger and whispered, "Do you think they got it by now?"

Roger glanced around. "I think so. The courier assured me it would be delivered by noon today." He smiled.

"I'm glad you thought of that. I'm sure the families of those guards can use all the help they can get. They'll never know who it came from."

They felt good contributing to the funds set up for the families of the guards killed in the robbery. They anonymously donated a large portion of the recovered money to those funds.

George returned. Emily, followed by Trixie, went back to the galley with Helen.

"Roger, you seem to be doing better now that your work has picked up," George said. "I must admit I was worried last winter. You seemed depressed. That's pretty understandable with being out of work for so long."

"You've got that right. I'm glad things have picked up, too. I was driving Emily crazy being underfoot all the time."

George nodded. "Helen couldn't stand having me around all the time. I couldn't stand being around her all the time. What a thought!"

Emily had the table set when Roger brought in the steaks.

"I'll open the champagne," Roger said.

Emily smiled and handed him a bottle of pink champagne. Roger popped the cork and let it fly into the sea. After he poured, everyone sat down at the table and began eating.

"Are you two planning anymore sailing trips?" Helen asked.

"Yes," Emily said. "We're going to take the whole month of August and sail along the coast of Maine. There are some beautiful spots."

"I envy you," George said. "You're smart to take the time to enjoy yourselves. No sense working all the time, when you have the opportunity to do things like that."

"George, are you suggesting we should take some trips?" Helen asked, smiling.

"Oh no, now I've got myself in trouble," he grinned.

"We're glad you two could come out this weekend," Emily said.

Roger agreed and proposed a toast. "To family and friends. It's great when the two are the same."

They laughed and toasted with him.

The cellular phone rang.

"Who'd call us here on Sunday?" Emily asked. "I'll get it."

"Stay put, Em," Roger said. "I'll answer it."

He stood back from the table and reached for the phone. "Hello?"

"Roger, this is Smitty. How's the boat?"

"Nice to hear from you, Smitty. Is everything all right?"

"Just wanted to let you know about that old well on the south side of your property."

Roger almost choked. "The well?"

Emily looked up in alarm. Roger hadn't filled it in yet. They decided to wait a few months so they wouldn't draw attention to it while Detective Hayes was still around.

"Yeah," Smitty said. "Don't worry. I took care of it for you, and it's all filled in and covered over. No one willl know it was ever there."

"You did?" Roger was too stunned to think of anything else to say.

"Are you all right?" Smitty asked.

"Yeah. Thanks, Smitty. I've been meaning to do that for a long time."

"I figured you were. It's not safe to have an old well around like that. You never know what or who might fall in."

Roger frowned and imagined that devilish twinkle in Smitty's eyes. "You're right. Any problems?"

"Not a bit. I filled it in, then piled rocks over it. It's no danger to anyone now. I just thought I'd better let you know. You folks enjoy your stay on the island. Everything's fine back here."

"Thanks, Smitty. I appreciate it."

"Don't mention it. By the way, I've got some venison in the freezer for you when you get back."

"Did you get that buck?"

Smitty laughed. "No, he's still here. Too crafty for me. He's waiting for you next hunting season. He ain't done tormenting you yet."

Roger smiled. "Thanks. We'll see you when we get home."

"Sure thing."

Emily glanced at Roger, guessing all was well. Roger winked at her as he turned off the phone and returned to the table.

"How about another toast?" George offered. "To friends."

"To friends!" Roger raised his glass and smiled.

the end

Happy Sails II U